Home to the Sea

Brown Barn Books
Weston, Connecticut

Home to the Sea

by
Chester Aaron

Brown Barn Books
Weston, Connecticut

Brown Barn Books,
A division of Pictures of Record, Inc.
119 Kettle Creek Road, Weston, Connecticut 06883, U.S.A.
www.brownbarnbooks.com

HOME TO THE SEA
Copyright © 2004 by Chester Aaron

Library of Congress Control Number: 2004104780
ISBN 0-9746481-2-4

Aaron, Chester.

HOME TO THE SEA: a novel by Chester Aaron

Printed in the United States of America

To the dedicated volunteers,
past and present,
at the Marine Mammal Center
in Sausalito, California.

They give not just their time
but their bodies, hearts and minds.

1

"I am not sick," Marian said.

Her mother held the thermometer in the air, adjusted her glasses, frowned, and thinking natural light might help, moved closer to the window. Troubled, she handed the thermometer to Marian's father, Robert.

Muttering something about never being able to read thermometers, he held this one close to his eyes and squinted. Finally, after staring at the column of mercury and the numbers and then staring at Marian, and still failing to connect the message of the thermometer to his daughter lying there in her bed, he shifted his attention to his wife. "Evelyn, am I reading this thing right? I'm either holding it upside down or it's broken. Or Marian's been sleeping in the freezer."

Evelyn Conroy felt her daughter's forehead. "When Marian Conroy turns up her nose at a hamburger, she's sick. I better call Ted."

"I'm not sick, Mom. I just looked at that hamburger and saw some poor innocent cow all chopped up. And I didn't *turn up my nose*."

"That hamburger was rare last night and you always like your burgers charred. Maybe the rare did it."

"It was hamburger, Mom. Hamburger is meat. Animal meat. Please, I don't want to talk about it. Just talking about it makes me want to barf again."

"In your whole life you've never talked about a hamburger and barfed. Incidentally, when I was a kid we never barfed, we threw up. Do you realize how many hamburgers you have eaten in your twelve years without the slightest urge to barf?"

"Or throw up?" her father added.

"Three thousand four hundred and thirty-one," Marian said. "And a half. OK? No more. Not even a bite. And incidentally, I've been eating hamburgers for nine years. Not twelve. The first three years I ate baby food."

"Marian, you're being silly."

"You're in your vegetarian stage," her father said. "The vegetarian bug bites girls around the age of 13. It never bites boys. Two years from now the bug will be... what? The dessert-bug? Ooh, mom, no chocolate chip cookies. Next, you'll be obsessed with horses for two years. The horse-bug. After horses? Boys. The boy-bug. Then the makeup-bug, then the no-makeup-bug, the natural look-bug. Look, ma, I'm a farmgirl. I got manure on my shoes."

"Chocolate chip cookies? Wanna bet? You're not being fair, Dad."

"No one who knows me," Robert Conroy said, "will tell you I have ever been famous for being fair. Seriously, Mare, your mom and I are worried about you. I'm not trying to put you down when I say young girls go through phases. Old people do, too. Look at me. I went through a phase called youth."

"The geezer-bug bite you, Dad? What do *you* think...? Do I need Ted?"

"What do I think? I think you're a normal girl caught up in the latest fad. Veganism."

"I bet there's no such word as veganism. Is there, Mom?" asked Marian, grimacing, as if the image gave her a stomach-ache. "And what's a normal girl, Dad?"

"Your father's right. I'm calling Ted," her mother said, picking up the phone next to Marian's bed. "Hi, Pauline. Evelyn here. I know you just sat down to dinner but can I please talk to Ted for just a minute? Thanks."

Ted Longacre, their neighbor and their doctor, had delivered Marian almost thirteen years ago.

The Conroys had lived in this house on Cliffside Avenue, near San Francisco, for twenty years. In that period they and the Longacres had become very close friends. Two or three evenings a week, when schedules permitted, they had dinner together. They shared season tickets to the Post Street Theater and the San Francisco Opera, and once or twice a month, they drove to Berkeley for a dance performance or a lecture. Springs and summers they frequently drove north along the Pacific coast to Sonoma or Mendocino, usually in the Conroy's wagon, which could carry all of them. The car's roof had room enough for food and equipment for a beach cookout.

Marian heard her mother on the phone, describing the symptoms to Ted. "Robert might be right. The thermometer could be broken. But I'd appreciate...Oh, thanks, Ted." Then, hanging up the phone and turning to Robert and Marian, she said, "He's coming right over."

Marian wondered if she'd have to spend a few days in bed. If so, she knew what to expect. When one of the kids was sick, her mother would make their favorite sour-cream scones. Marian and her brothers ate them almost as fast as she could produce them. But this evening? The thought of chewing and swallowing those buttery balls of dough covered with jam almost provoked the same disastrous effects caused by last night's undercooked hamburger.

As the warmth from her mother's hand lingered on Marian's forehead, she squirmed a bit farther beneath her blanket to escape the unpleasantly warm hand. She had to admit she wasn't feeling great.

But it, whatever it was, would pass, as similar feelings had come and gone before. Twice before? No, once before. Nope, twice. And now and then hints of such feelings that didn't develop into major productions like last night and today. The first time, that was a bad one, she remembered.

How old had she been? Five? Six, maybe? Ted had come over late in the evening that time too, after dinner, to examine her.

Was this as bad as that time? Was she nauseated that time? Yeah. Big-time barf night. Her brothers Tommy and Todd had been home then and they had complained that she should use the downstairs bathroom so they couldn't hear her.

Had her back hurt as much as it was hurting now? And her legs, had they felt so stiff, so tingly? Yes, all that. All that and something else. She remembered now she'd had difficulty breathing then, as she'd had last night and this morning, as she was having right now.

"I'll find the vaporizer," Evelyn said. "Get a little humidity in the room."

"I bet it's the flu," Robert said. He'd said it then, too, that first time.

3

"That time of year," he said now as he'd said then. "I'll bet she has the flu."

That first time, after Ted Longacre had taken Marian's temperature and checked her throat and listened to her heart, he, like her father, had said, "It's the flu. She needs lots of rest, lots of fluids. Two children's aspirins in the morning, two in the evening. I bet she's fine by tomorrow morning."

He'd been right on. By breakfast the next morning she had recovered completely.

But this time, so far at least, the four aspirins she'd already taken had little effect. Her head still ached and she still had trouble breathing. Her lungs seemed too heavy for her body. There was something else, something new. Her fingers and toes, this very minute, were numb.

Maybe, Marian thought, she just wouldn't eat much today.

Actually, she hadn't eaten much yesterday, or the day before. Not much more, as far as she remembered, than some tea and graham crackers. But as weak as she'd been, she'd still beat Kathy Lumley home from school, even after Kathy had jumped on her bike and taken a lead of ten yards.

There had been one dangerous moment today, at lunch, when she followed Kathy through the school cafeteria line. The smell of hot dogs and baked beans had chased Marian to the bathroom. Kathy had followed her. As Marian had raced down the hall, Kathy had run after her, shouting, "Go, Mare, go...you'll make it, Mare...go."

She'd made it, barely.

〰〰

When Ted Longacre appeared he wasn't, for the moment, neighbor or friend. He was the doctor.

His black leather bag and the stethoscope draped around his neck made him look like one of those handsome television doctors. He now used that stethoscope as he'd used it five years ago, placing the rubber-capped tips in his ears and the metal disk first on Marian's bare chest and then on her back, moving it up and down and crosswise. "Breathe in... breathe out...breathe in...cough..."

Following an examination of her mouth, her teeth, her throat, her ears, Ted said, to Marian's mother and father, "Let's all of us sit down in the kitchen and have some coffee."

"Me, too?" Marian asked.

"Of course you too," Ted said.

Her mother helped Marian with her robe and, in the process, found time to hold her in her arms and kiss her cheek and murmur, "Don't be scared, baby."

No one said anything until the coffee was poured. Marian's mother, deciding not to sit, stood holding her cup.

Marian, hunched slightly forward, sipped her hot tea, even though she didn't want anything.

Ted said, "Bob, your thermometer isn't broken. Marian's temperature is low. Abnormally low. Almost dangerously low."

Marian didn't know what those words meant but they had to be serious because her mother's face grew very pale and her hands shook so badly she spilled the coffee. Robert reached over to steady Evelyn's hands. Then he gently pulled the cup free and set it on the table and eased her into her chair.

Marian had never seen fright on her father's face but there it was: in his wide eyes, in his tight lips, in his trembling hands.

Ted said, "I'm taking Marian to the hospital. I want you both to go with me."

Robert glanced at his watch. "When?"

"In an hour. Give me time to have some dinner. I'll call in and order an x-ray of Marian's chest this evening and some lab work."

Robert shook his head, as if to mix his random thoughts into order. "But she's the picture of health, Ted. Look at her."

Evelyn, got up and placed a hand on Marian's shoulder. "You're not putting her in the hospital, are you, Ted? She's not that sick, is she?"

Ted started to reassure Evelyn but then, seeming to think better of it, said, "Maybe you ought to pack a few things, Marian. Just in case."

〰
〰

After the x technician brought the x-ray films into the radiologist's office and slapped them onto the illuminated viewing glass, Dr. Longacre and the radiologist discussed the films, a murmured discussion Marian and her parents, sitting in the waiting room, could barely hear.

Then Ted came out and invited them to join him in the radiologist's office. They followed him. Ted introduced them to the tall blond woman who had a soft Southern drawl. "This is Dr. Kaplan," Ted said. "She's a radiologist; she interprets x-ray films," he told Marian. "She wasn't here five years ago but we have those films we did then for comparison."

Dr. Kaplan asked Marian to lower her robe to her waist. Using her own stethoscope, she examined a variety of locations on Marian's chest and back. For perhaps five minutes Marian answered Dr. Kaplan's questions, breathed as she was directed, stuck out her tongue, and watched the radiologist return to study the films on the viewing-screens. Pointing here and there, as she and Ted discussed the patterns of lights and shadows, Dr. Kaplan never raised her voice above a whisper. But Marian and her mother and father heard the words *pneumonia* and *pleurisy* and, again, *edema* and *bronchial* and, three or four times, the phrase *lungs filled with fluid*.

Finally, Ted turned to Evelyn and Robert Conroy. "I have to tell you. Unlike every other patient I have seen with edematous lungs... sorry...lungs filled with fluid, Marian doesn't have even the slightest difficulty breathing. Her films from five years ago showed no fluid. The lungs were clear. But I'm concerned, as is Dr. Kaplan, because we both see and hear fluid in her lungs this time. Normally, patients with lungs that demonstrate such a condition can barely stand, let alone be rational. Marian isn't just rational, she's completely coordinated physically. She doesn't appear sick enough to be admitted to the hospital but we have to know not just the source of that fluid but its composition. So..."

Evelyn and Robert Conroy waited. Marian was wondering if she could take the x-rays home to show Kathy Lumley.

"So what, Ted?" Robert asked.

"Let me tell you something else. Normal body temperature, as you know, is 98.6. A child of Marian's age—forgive me, Mare, you're twelve years old, so in my book you're still a child—a child might vary a degree or two either way. But 17 degrees? I've used three different thermometers and Dr. Kaplan has used her own. All four have registered an extremely abnormal 81.7 degrees. I want Marian to stay in the hospital tonight for lab work and other tests, like an EKG and maybe even a bone scan. I've called in Dr. Gross, an endocrinologist, to consult. I'm sure he'll want to do some tests of his own tonight and possibly tomorrow."

Evelyn and Robert, trying, for Marian's sake, to appear nonchalant, said that if Ted thought that was the best thing to do, then that was what would be done. They hugged Marian and told her they would both return early in the morning. Did she want them to bring anything special? Books, toothpaste, anything?

Marian, said she'd brought everything she needed for an overnight and seemed to accept her fate with uncommon good humor.

"Look at her," Ted said. "She looks like she's ready to race Kathy Lumley down the street. Oh yes, Marian, we saw the two of you."

Marian didn't say that right this minute she didn't exactly feel as healthy as she looked. Should she tell them about the new pain in her stomach? No, no need. That was probably caused by drinking so much ice water.

After the admissions nurse appeared and after the various papers were signed, Marian was fastened into a wheelchair, despite her complaints that she could walk.

After kissing her mother and father she said there was nothing to worry about. In fact, she herself was beginning to see the entire event as an adventure, one her brothers, away at college, would miss.. "You have to call Tommy and Todd," Marian said, "and tell them I'm in the hospital."

"Certainly," Evelyn said. "But you know them. Don't expect a *get well* card or even a call."

Marian managed a smile and a brief chuckle. "They'll be jealous. They're always having the adventures. They go to baseball games, they've been to Disneyland, they've flown across the country to visit Grandma Audrey. But they've never been a patient in a hospital with a weird temperature and fluid in their heads."

"Their lungs," Evelyn said.

Marian, laughing, said, "Whatever, Mom."

"I'll call them tonight," Robert said. "I'll lay it on. I'll tell them Dr. Whoozey on TV is coming in to interview you and you're getting four transplants."

Her brothers, Marian knew, would pretend to be cool about the whole thing but she also knew they would envy her. They better. She could hardly wait for her mother and father to leave so this adventure could begin.

"Oh," she added, "call Kathy. Tell her I'm subnormal and I can have visitors."

"Abnormal," said the nurse, waiting patiently for an appropriate time to escape the parents and rush off with her patient.

"Let's have a no-visitor period," Ted said. "Your mom and dad, OK. But no one else. Not yet."

"You think she has something contagious?" Evelyn said.

"We're just being cautious, Ev. An outsider can bring bugs in as well as take bugs out. We'll be cautious until tomorrow."

"OK, but please call Kathy and tell her we'll talk tomorrow."

♒︎

Late the next afternoon, Ted told Marian's parents that the various exams had verified the presence of serious levels of fluid in Marian's lungs, though, thank goodness, this morning's follow-up studies, especially the x-rays, showed the lungs to be much clearer than they had appeared last night.

Dr. Gross, the endocrinologist, had examined Marian and the results of the tests he'd ordered indicated that though there were some questions about her blood chemistry, there was nothing serious enough to keep her in the hospital. Yes, she could now go home.

"We'll talk," Ted said. "But I want you to know that from here on, for at least a year or two, I'll want Marian in the hospital for a series of tests every four months. Any problem with that?"

All three Conroys shook their heads. No problem.

Speaking directly to Marian, after kissing her on the nose, Ted said, "Most kids with these kinds of problems outgrow them, Marian. You will too. Is that a promise?"

"That's a promise, Ted," Marian said, as she reached up to pull his face down so she might kiss the tip of *his* nose.

"Dr. Longacre to you," Ted said. He tenderly gathered a handful of Marian's hair and shook her head, as if to rearrange the material inside. "Mare, you know that Pauline and I love you almost as much as these two guys who claim they're your parents."

~~~

Ted insisted that Marian stay in bed through the weekend.

"You both work—but I know a retired pediatric nurse who can stay with her. Her name is Mrs. Kearns. Here's her number. Call her the minute you get home."

In the car, on the way home, Marian said, "Did you tell Tommy and Todd?"

"Of course," her mother said.

"And?"

"They send you their love."

"That's all?"

"Well, Tommy said something about you snoring and keeping every patient on your floor awake all night."

"I don't snore," Marian declared. Then, unsure, she asked, "Do I?"

"To tell the truth," her mother said, "you do. Especially when it's warm. I suspect it's allergies. We'll talk to Ted about that."

"Ooh, I hate snoring. I can hear Daddy sometimes and it's so gross."

"I never snore," Robert said. "I just breathe in deeper than most people."

"Believe me," Evelyn said. "I'm a mathematician. To me facts are truths. And I say it's a fact you snore."

Marian stretched out on the backseat on the way home, and she could see her father peering into the rearview mirror to observe her face. "Mare, guess what else Todd said when we called them."

" 'Shove a hamburger down her throat.' "

"You got it," Robert said. "Word-for-word."

Audrey Gibson, Marian's grandmother, called from Maine shortly after dinner the next Friday night. She'd called, she said, on impulse. She'd talked to Robert and Evelyn the last few times she'd called, and Tommy and Todd had visited her there in Maine, but tonight she had a sudden need to talk to her granddaughter.

"Well," Evelyn told her mother, "your intuition is, as usual, impressive. I'll get her. Marian, you should know, has been in the hospital."

Grandma Audrey waited for more, but Evelyn said, "I'll get Marian. You can hear it from the horse's mouth."

"Hi, Grandma, I guess this is the horse's mouth," Marian said, trying to control herself so her somewhat staid grandma wouldn't think she was too silly.

"Your mother tells me you've been in the hospital."

"For one night and one day. I'm fine now, Grandma."

"What was so serious, child, that required you go to a hospital?"

Marian, perceiving in her grandmother's voice a tone of serious concern, described the symptoms that had followed her nausea after the hamburger—aches in her joints, sharp pains in her back, and an aversion to heat. "It's winter but every morning when I wake up I've kicked off my blankets. I keep turning the thermostat down and Mrs. Kearns keeps turning it back up."

"Mrs. Kearns?"

"She's a nurse. She's been staying in my room. She sleeps on a cot. Ted, our neighbor…"

"The doctor. I've met them, him and his wife. A very impressive couple. I'm so relieved you have them next door."

"He's taken care of me ever since I was born. In fact, he delivered me. Anyway, when I came home, he said I had to have someone—a nurse—in the house when Mom and Dad aren't here. But she, I mean Mrs. Kearns, keeps turning the thermostat up and I keep turning it down."

Audrey Bishop had remained quiet during Marian's cataloging of the details of her illness but now she asked, "Is it more severe this time than it was the last time, five years ago?"

The last time.

No, she hadn't been so sick the last time, and she hadn't gone to the hospital. The diagnosis that time had been the flu. This time there had been no diagnosis.

"I was a lot sicker this time, Grandma. Ted thinks it might have been one of those new kinds of flu from Asia or somewhere."

"You weren't nauseated the last time."

"I wasn't? Oh, you remembered. No, I guess I wasn't. You remember better than I do. But this time it's winter, so it's colder and that makes it easier. When I'm cold my bones don't hurt so much. In fact I feel better when the air's cold."

Marian and her grandmother talked for almost an hour. During the conversation Audrey Bishop confided that she too, when she was a girl, had often gone for days without eating anything but fish. Did Marian like fish?

"I could eat tuna for every meal, Grandma. And clam chowder. Mom makes the best clam chowder in the world."

"She should if she's still using my recipe. Wait until you come to Maine, darling. I'll show you what the word *chowder* means. Now, about that visit. I'm going to work on your mother. I'd love to have you visit me this summer but I suspect she will fight that idea."

"Oh, Grandma, please do. Please please please."

"I'll try but I've tried before. We haven't been lucky, you and I. No problem with the boys, their coming here to the house didn't bother Evelyn. But the idea of you spending time with your grandmother is...well, it has always been awkward. I exaggerate. You're so much younger than the boys."

"But it's still not fair. Tommy and Todd get to do all sorts of things because they're older but mostly because they're boys."

"Say no more. This isn't a gender issue. But we, you and I, shall keep trying. I want to spend more than just an occasional hour with my favorite grandchild every other year, which is what happens when I'm there in California. Now don't you dare tell your brothers I said that."

"About me being your favorite grandchild?"

"Precisely."

"Aw, Grandma, please. I can just see their faces."

"Marian Conroy, you be discreet. You have to protect me from my own indiscretions."

"What're *indiscretions*?"

"You look it up in the dictionary, child. I mean Marian."

When Marian had come home from the hospital, she had refused to snip the plastic band from her wrist. As her brothers sat near her bed, she flashed her wrist-band in their faces. She also let them know that Grandma Audrey had called to talk to her and had invited her to come to Maine very soon.

Todd said Marian would be spooked by Grandma Audrey's house so she better wait for twelve more years before she visited, she better "...you know, maybe grow up a little, be more mature."

Tommy said he thought Grandma Audrey's house might be haunted. "Honest to God, Mare, I mean really really haunted."

"Grandma will never admit it," Todd said, "but I kept hearing strange noises all night. Coming from different rooms. Uncle Talbot's house, too. Now there—Uncle Talbot's house—is a place I wouldn't sleep in without a platoon of bodyguards."

"You guys aren't scaring me, so quit trying."

The boys agreed that the best times back in Maine had been the days they spent with their eccentric uncle on his fishing boat. He'd died since their last visit, so Marian would never meet him. Their agreement, Marian knew, was pure theater presented just to tease. *Go ahead*, she thought but didn't say, *make me jealous, just try.*

"He's weird, isn't he, Tom? And that house?"

"Weird weird weird. He ain't with us no mo no mo. Yeah, he was wild, Todd. That house? Spooky, man. Spoo-ookey."

Tommy dragged out the last word and sang it while shaking his head and snapping his fingers as if in accompaniment to music only he could hear.

Todd shook and nodded, picking up the same rhythm, the same head-bob and finger-snap, and then said seriously, "Grandma called him eccentric."

Tommy, imitating Grandma Audrey, said, "In a family of eccentrics your Uncle Talbot is the prizewinner."

"Eccentric?" Marian asked.

"Eccentric like *weird*," Tommy said.

Todd, grinning, said, "Like *spooky*. I kept sneezing when we got close to him. I think he had more dust on him than on his desk. The only thing that wasn't covered with dust was his boat."

"You know the name he gave his boat, Mare?"

She waited.

"Merman."

"After that singer," Tommy said. "That Broadway singer. Her name was Ethel Merman."

So? Marian thought but didn't say.

"Remember that story?" Todd asked, forcing himself not to look at Marian to guarantee her continuing interest.

"The submarine?"

"Yeah." Tommy let the next word hang in limbo, knowing Marian would be unable to restrain her curiosity.

"What?" she asked, hating herself for submitting.

"It was just a story, Mare."

"Come on, Todd. What was the story?"

"OK. He was in the Vietnam war, right? In the navy. In a submarine. You know about submarines?"

"I know about submarines. So?"

Todd, laughing as he pretended to try to remember, said, "Uncle Talbot tells us this loopy story about...What was it, Tom? What did he call it?"

"A merrow. Like in bone marrow. Was that it? Was that the word?"

"Yeah. He said he read this story about a guy who was in a sub under the ice at the North Pole and their equipment picks up these strange sounds they can't get a fix on and the captain thinks it's some trick by the

Vietnamese because the imaging equipment identifies it as a human voice outside the sub in the icy water. A human voice."

"And it was singing."

"Yeah. In English, I guess. Maybe Vietnamese."

"That was the story?"

"Well, that's not the end of it. Uncle Talbot told us he had the very same experience the guy in the story had. Uncle Talbot was the sonar guy on his sub and there were some strange sounds and the image the sonar gave was a voice, a human female voice. It was a merrow outside the sub and he knew it was a merrow because of the image on the screen. The merrow was swimming right against the submarine."

Marian waited, her skin beginning to itch and then to burn. Why did she know, before she even asked the question, what the answer would be?

"What's a merrow?" she asked, barely above a whisper.

Tommy laughed as he looked to Todd for support. "Where? Scotland? This merrow's from Scotland, right?"

"Ireland. In Ireland when a sailor sees a merrow it means there are big storms coming so seeing a merrow's bad luck. And when we asked Uncle Talbot what a merrow is he..."

Marian's words escaped her dry throat. "A merrow's a mermaid."

The laughter Todd and Tommy had been sharing was silenced.

"How'd you know that?" Todd said, annoyed at her ending their game.

Marian's reply was a shrug, a slow shake of her head. She would have answered his question if she knew the answer.

Tommy, trying to revive their game, said, "Too bad Uncle Talbot died and you won't ever get to meet him, Mare. He was a character. Even Mom rolls her eyes when we talk about him."

While Marian was trying to get the sudden flood of memories into focus and into order, trying to locate the image of her uncle stored somewhere in those memories, Todd, stomping and swaying and bobbing his head in his own version of a ghetto-rapper, chanted, "Sister Marian, you and me, we got family they full of pee, we got this uncle, he's a real nut-cake, we got this grandma..."

Marian almost leaped at him. "Don't you dare make fun of Grandma."

Realizing he had entered dangerous territory, Todd decided to stop the comedy. He nodded at Tommy, and both brothers moved toward the door.

Marian's voice stopped them. "Did you tell Mom all that, about Uncle Talbot and the merrow?"

They paused long enough for Tommy to say, "Yeah," and for Todd to add, "We tried to."

"You know Mom. Mathematicians…" Tommy explained.

"He's her brother," Marian whispered.

"Was her brother."

And Todd, shuffling his feet, said, "I don't think they got along."

"Did…Grandma…did Grandma Audrey say that?"

"No, no. It's just that…well, Mom said something like, 'My brother was always an eccentric.' Something like that."

"Mom's a mathematician, Mare. They laugh at stuff like merrows and haunted houses and ghosts."

Marian closed her eyes and lay back. Maybe they'd think she was going to sleep. But she wasn't sleeping. She had located, in that vast reservoir of tangled images, the memory of Uncle Talbot.

By Saturday night, Marian was so bored with Mrs. Kearns, the nurse, she pretended to sleep so they'd not have to talk.

Her brothers fulfilled their obligations by staying with her for 15 minutes each day, sitting still the first five minutes and spending the next ten edging toward the door.

Sunday night, after the nurse had left, Ted Longacre examined Marian. He could find no evidence of fluid in her lungs, and her temperature was 98.4 degrees.

Even so, Ted suggested Marian suffer through one more day of bedrest. But yes, Kathy Lumley could visit that night.

"Did Mrs. Kearns work out, Marian?"

Marian crossed her fingers beneath the blankets when she said, "She helped a lot."

"I don't think you need her any more. Even when your mom and dad aren't here. You can take care of yourself now. You agree?"

"I…well, let me think…I…well, OK. I agree."

Ted laughed. "You're as transparent as that window, Mare."

Marian and Kathy would have nothing to say to each other that night, Robert said at the dinner table, because they'd been exchanging five or six calls every day and gossiping for hours each time. "Nothing's left to talk about," he said.

"Want to bet, Dad?"

〰

Sunday. Midnight.

Marian stirred beneath her thin blanket and sat up.

Quick sharp stabs of cold air brought a flush to her face. Why was she so alert?

Something or someone had wakened her, had been calling to her to get out of bed.

Beyond where Mrs. Kearns' cot would have been, Marian saw the sliding glass door and the darkness beyond.

There! The call came again.

Marian slipped free of her blanket.

The usually noisy floorboards were silent as Marian crossed the room and silently opened the sliding door. Outside, the howling wind that had been rattling the windows a moment before was now an ally, grown suddenly quiet as she left the oceanfront house.

Marian picked her way through beds of dried grass, avoiding the rocks that could bruise a toe or turn an ankle.

There!

From the dark space below the call came again.

She hurried toward the sound, descending through the terraced beds of shrubs and weeds toward the path cut long ago into the side of the cliff.

The next call, hurled forward by the wind, was louder than the sound of surf pounding the beach below. Marian moved toward that sound as if it was pulling her out from the land.

With the agility of a cat, Marian was up and over the fence and then running, sliding, down the path.

Standing finally on a flat shelf of rock above the sand, she looked down at the tide rolling toward her and the surf foaming in the light of the moon and stars. She breathed in the scent of the ocean. Had the ocean ever smelled or tasted so sweet, so delicious, so nourishing?

She stepped down from the rock shelf to the sand. The receding tide caught and pulled her feet from under her. She sat and slid on the thick mud-slush to firmer foam-washed sand where she could stand up. She walked toward the breaking surf, pulling off her nightgown and tossing it back over her head. Naked, she ran across the sand until the incoming tide reached her ankles and then her knees. She arched her body and entered the advancing waves headfirst, arms at her sides. Her laughter, like a song, greeted the ocean as if it were a more familiar force in her life than land had ever been.

There!

The calls were closer now and clearer, variations of pitch and tone that rose, more distinct, above the sounds of surf and wind to form an almost solid tapestry of nonhuman voices that floated across the waves.

Marian wasn't sure if she was above the water, moving over it, or deep below, slipping through it.

Her arms and legs stopped moving and she floated, yielding to the waves. Then, swimming again, she rushed beyond the breaking waves into an endless stretch of smooth placid water. Her eyes seemed to reflect huge dollops of the moon's white light.

The lights on land were lost now. There was only the moon and the stars and the night.

She might have slept there in the water had the calls not again come from the sea, chasing each other around her floating body—an undulating chorus of high-pitched, sharp-edged songs precise as bird calls, starting in low tones and rising to a pitch so high her ears ached in response. Guttural sounds replaced the high sharp calls to be replaced in turn by an occasional but clearly audible series of clicks, long sentences composed of clicks.

Here then was the source of the calls that had called her from the house and guided her down the side of the cliff to the water. The calls came from the denizens of these waters, the beasts she could feel now all around her, could even see, now and then. Floating islands hurled from the bottom of the ocean up to the surface of the water, some of them towering above her, some of them moving beneath her, many lying close beside her. As they frolicked around her, Marian felt a joy she knew she had never known before and would never ever know on land when she returned.

These ocean creatures were offering themselves to her as friends, as brothers, as sisters.

One and then another of the creatures drifted beneath her and, rising, lifted her clear of the water. As they moved her, as they carried her through the wind and then deposited her gently inside the troughs that followed each of the rolling waves, she could see, in the moonlight, a vast armada of other sleek bodies gathered to welcome her into their world.

Now one body moved up beneath her, lifted her higher, turned her, carried her toward shore.

Another arrived to share the journey, to lift her and carry her farther.

And a third and a fourth. Lifted, carried.

Specks popped out of the darkness.

Lights, she realized, of cars. Cars on the highway that paralleled the shore.

The specks grew brighter, larger. Now she could see the moonlight on the beach and then there was the cliff capped by the silhouette of her dark home. Her friends were bringing her from their home to hers.

The closer she was to shore the less audible grew the calls of her new sea friends. The sounds weakened, grew infrequent, ceased.

With a sigh that could have come from either of them, Marian slid down from her mount. Her hands, as she dropped across the body, moved over the fins, down over the head to a mouth that caught and held the fingers for a brief moist moment.

Then she was swimming alone.

Standing finally in the sea foam, she walked forward onto the firm sand. Here was her nightgown, spread like a forlorn white butterfly. She picked it up.

Here was the path.

Here were the steps. The gate.

Here was the glass door, still open.

She closed the door behind her, locked it, crossed the room. Her nightgown dropped to the floor. She slipped beneath the blanket.

The wind rose, to scream and shake the windows and doors inside their frames.

≋

Near sunrise Evelyn Conroy turned on the light, hurried to Marian's bed and felt her forehead, her cheek, her hair. Gasping at the wet hair, she stepped back, stifling a scream. The sheet that covered Marian was smeared with what Evelyn thought at first was blood but then, as she spread the sheet, was, she realized, mud.

No matter how hard she tried, Evelyn couldn't waken Marian from her sleep to guide her to the shower. She did the next best thing, bringing basin after basin of hot soapy water to wash Marian's feet and hands and pale body.

Throughout the replacement of soiled linen with clean, the soft rub of the thick towel, and the roll of her body back and forth, Marian remained asleep and even smiled.. Twice Evelyn was sure she heard the word *love* and the word *kiss*.

≋

An energetic, smiling Marian bounced into her parents' bedroom before the alarm clock buzzed.

"Good morning," she sang. "Come on, let's have breakfast. I'm hungry."

Marian's appetite, not quite satisfied by three soft-boiled eggs and four slices of toast and two mugs of hot chocolate, made her mother and father smile with relief.

When Kathy Lumley rang the bell and accepted a muffin and Marian grabbed her books, the two of them, laughing and bumping each other, went off to school as if Marian hadn't missed a single moment of a single class.

Ted Longacre decided not to tell the Conroys that he noticed barely visible irregularities in Marian's spine and that Dr. Gross, the endocrinologist, had been concerned about possible abnormalities in Marian's pituitary gland. Dr. Longacre had been so concerned that he'd sent copies of all the x-rays and medical reports to specialists at several research institutions.

Within days, phone calls, letters and e-mails were confirming his early fears of those first few days when he had examined Marian and packed her off to the hospital. The unanimous opinion, stated in variations of medical terminology: *This patient is extremely ill; death is imminent.*

Several weeks later, Dr. Longacre informed his esteemed colleagues that the patient hadn't died. In fact, the patient was so far from death that she was now playing on the soccer team. The patient also had a new Italian mountain bike.

Dr. Longacre's esteemed colleagues angrily charged him with sending them x-rays and medical records of another patient with Marian Conroy's name mistakenly applied. Possibly, they argued, not wishing to offend a fellow physician, it had been the hospital's fault. After all, record departments in all hospitals, public and private, are notoriously inefficient.

〰

Marian told no one, not even Kathy Lumley, about her moonlight swim and the calls of the sea beasts. She certainly couldn't tell her mother and father, though she often caught her mother watching her as if an explanation for some undefined but erratic behavior was in order.

The experience of that night was buried so deep in her memory that when she talked to her grandmother several days later she didn't even think to mention the incident. Nor did she think to mention it to Kathy, her dearest friend and confidante.

Kathy, like all the others, family and friends, knew that Marian had never been permitted to venture alone into even the shallowest pool.

The ocean at the bottom of the cliff?

Forget it.

And there was another reason for doubt.

Marian had never learned to swim.

On a Friday night in late April, almost two months after she had been declared doomed by various medical experts, Marian lounged on her bed with her best friend Kathy, weighing the merits of being Marian Conroy or Kathy Lumley against the benefits of being Britney or Madonna.

After they talked about what they liked and didn't like about themselves—hair, eyes, noses, voices, favorite music and/or singers, movies, TV shows, friends (not counting each other of course), and favorite enemies—after all the exchanges and comparisons, both admitted they liked the other's parents better.

Perhaps *like* wasn't the right word.

Felt easier with was better.

Or *could talk to.*

Or *could always expect a joke from.*

Or *just didn't have to say "Excuse me? You listening to me?"* to.

"One thing though," Kathy said, beginning a complaint Marian had been hearing ever since meeting her in third grade. "Your mom and dad don't make you eat health food, which I hate! Hate! Hate!"

Kathy said *health food* as if it were another word for laxative and Marian wondered why it was called health food because when she ate at Kathy's house she always felt sick afterwards.

"You get to eat all the good stuff, Mare. My mom and dad never buy potato chips or soda and I love potato chips and my dream is to fill my bathtub with soda and lie there all day swallowing the bathwater."

Laughter. Pounding of pillows.

"There's not even a raisin in the house that isn't organic." Kathy spoke the word *organic* as if it tasted bad in her mouth. "And tofu. You ever eat tofu? We eat fried tofu (fried in lettuce oil or something), baked tofu, boiled tofu, tofu desserts with special organic tofu-honey. You know what tofu tastes like, Mare? Boiled slugs. You're lucky to have your mom and dad. They are very *very* cool."

Marian did agree that her father was one of the funniest men ever. "Sometimes Mom screams when he jokes too much. Todd and Tommy love it; they make jokes and Mom just groans and sits there and looks at me and rolls her eyes and when I roll my eyes too she takes for granted I agree with her, which I don't. But you know what *you* get that I don't get and wish I did?"

"Tofu?"

Laughter to the point of tears. Pillow pounding.

"No," Marian said, after drying her eyes. "You get to do things like riding lessons. I'd love to ride horses. And swimming. You take swimming lessons so you get to go in the ocean and pools. I can't even take a bath unless Mom's standing there. She thinks I'll slip down through the drain and drown if I'm by myself. I have to take showers. I don't hate showers I just wish I didn't have Mom reminding me all the time to shower all the time. '*Why are you filling the tub, Marian, when you have this big beautiful shower?*' That was when we were in some motel in Santa Maria one night."

Kathy, laughing: "The only time I shower at home is when I use my mother's perfume. It's patchouli oil. Sounds like you're sneezing when you say it. Patchouli oil! Oh, God bless you!"

Laughter, more pounding of pillows.

"Your dad can fix things," Marian said. "He has all sorts of tools and machinery. He fixed my bike, remember? And that desk he built for Mom's computer is better than you could buy in any store. She said so and she knows."

"Well, yeah," Kathy said. "But I wish my parents read books. Look at all the books in your house. And your dad *writes* books. You're like him, you read all the time. I bet when you're old you'll write books. You've got more books here in your room than our school library."

Marian rushed to inject equal praise for her mother. "Mom teaches something called calculus at the university in Berkeley. It's sort of fancy arithmetic. And she's writing a book about mathematics. The book looks weird. Pages of nothing but numbers and symbols. Dad said it might as well be written in...I forget the language he said. Sandspit or something."

"Which one do you like best? Your dad or your mom?"

Marian stalled, pretending to be confused by the question. She didn't want to have to make a choice. "Which what?"

"Your mom or your dad?"

"Well, it's easier to get away with things with Dad. When he gets mad it's only for a minute or two. When Mom gets mad it's all day, sometimes a hundred days. Like when she hears I was at the beach. I've lived three hundred feet from the beach all my life and you know how many times I've been in the surf? I bet five, maybe six times. And always with Mom standing guard."

Kathy moved closer, as if fearing there might be someone else in the room who would overhear her. "Do your mom and dad fight? I mean like hurt each other? My uncle, Dad's brother, hits my aunt, his wife. He really hurts her. Dad won't let him in our house. They're very mad at each other. Mom says my uncle's a wife-beater because he doesn't eat organic food. She says if he had tofu every day..."

After some uncomfortable laughter they swerved into a new topic—the summer.

"Six more weeks," Kathy said. "First week of vacation I have a swim meet so Coach is really working me hard. He says, 'Kathy, if you want it bad enough you could go to the Olympics. But you've got to want it.' Hey! I have a two-hour session tomorrow at the pool and it's Saturday. Come with me, Mare. Mom'll pick you up. No one'll tell."

"Where is it?"

"The pool at Merrimac High School. Twenty minutes from here. I have to work on my backstroke."

"So I just sit there and watch Kathy Lumley work on her backstroke? No thanks. I'd rather...what's Dad say?...I'd rather watch grass grow."

"Hey, you could go in the pool if you want. Your mom won't be there."

"I'll tell you a big fat secret. I can't go in any pool. With or without Mom. Orders. From Mom. I don't even own a bathing suit. 'When you're sixteen,' my mom says. She used to say, 'when you're fourteen.' Then it was 'when you're fifteen.' Now it's 'when you're sixteen'. "

Kathy gasped. "You've never been in a pool? And you don't own...Mare, come on. Do it. Tell your mom we're going to the library. My mom'll pick you up and I'll bring an extra suit for you. Your mom'll never know."

Marian closed her eyes. The thought of immersion in water gave her goose bumps and sent strange little spasms along her legs. But lie to her mother? "OK," she said. "But only if you stay for dinner. Call and ask your mom if you can stay."

"That's not fair. You know..."

"If you lie to your mom I'll lie to my mom. Tell your mom we're having a special tofu dinner just to try it and if we like it we'll eat it forever."

"OK."

Marian stood beside Kathy while she phoned home, crossing her fingers, legs, and eyes.

Kathy's mother reluctantly said yes, and Marian and Kathy exchanged high-fives twice. "That's high-tens," Marian said.

〜〜

Both Tommy and Todd were home from college for the weekend. Kathy, uneasy in their presence, sighed with relief when Marian's mother set up a separate cardtable on the patio. "You two can watch the ocean," Evelyn said. "We're going to talk dull stuff inside. You'd be bored."

"Dull stuff? Like what?" Marian asked. "Calculus?"

"No. Your brothers have to start thinking about graduate school. Do they want to go? If they do, where? If they do, why?"

When Evelyn told the boys there was going to be pasta for dinner instead of the steaks they had been promised, they urged the discussion about graduate school be put off until morning.

"Yeah." Tommy said, "We can drive over to Pete Wiley's and have burgers and see a video. He has *Top Gun*."

"*Top Gun*," their father said. "Fighter pilots. The dream of every young American male who will never go to war. How many times have you seen it?"

"Seven," Todd said.

26

"Eight," Tommy whispered.

On the patio, gulping down a second serving of Evelyn's spaghetti and meatballs, Kathy whispered, "Mare, you ever wish you were a boy?"

"Never. Except when they get special treatment which they always do."

Kathy waited.

"They get to do things, go places girls don't. At least I don't."

Kathy waited.

"Five or six years ago they got to visit Grandma in Maine. That was the second time they went."

"So they visited your grandma six years ago?"

"Yeah. Six."

"So they were fifteen then. You're not thriteen yet. Soon, but not yet. Will you *ever* visit your grandma? Maybe when you're ninety?"

"I hope so. I love her. When she comes here we have special talks, just the two of us. She says we talk about things she doesn't talk about with anyone else in the family."

"Like what? What things?"

"Oh, like ghost stories and old-timey things." Marian held out both of her hands. "And stuff like this."

"What's that?" Kathy asked. "I've never seen that before. That's weird."

"I never showed you and you never looked. They're scars from surgery when I was a baby."

"Surgery for what? Let me see again."

Marian held out her hands and spread her fingers. "It's a very rare thing that happens to maybe one in a million babies. It's not dangerous but it's like…it's weird. When I was born I had this skin between my fingers. When it happens, the webs are usually gone before the person's a teenager. Mom didn't want to wait, she wanted it taken off my hands right away."

"But it's not all gone."

"It's just a little bit."

"You're one in a million?"

"Maybe it's one in two million. I forget. It's got a name but I forget what it is. It's a big scientific word."

"And you and you grandma talk about stuff like that?"

"Well, yeah, because she had this same skin thing when she was born. She grew out of it, she said, when she was fifteen. It was all gone by then."

"Toes too? Weird," Kathy said. "We've been friends forever and I never knew you had webbed toes." She laughed. "I'll call you Ducky from now on."

"You do," Marian said, "and I'll tell your mom and dad you've been eating potato chips and drinking Pepsi and Coke. Oh yeah. I remember what it's called. Syndatyly."

Kathy laughed. "Ductalee? Like a *duck-ta-lee*?"

When Marian didn't laugh, Kathy grew serious, then reached out and held Marian's hand. "I wish I was one in a million," she said.

"I think it was two million."

"I wish I was one in even a hundred, Mare."

〰

After the boys left the house, Evelyn said to the girls, "You guys go on. Marian, you can walk Kathy home but come right back."

As they cleaned up the kitchen, Evelyn and Robert Conroy discussed plans for the approaching summer. Tommy and Todd, with problems resolved, were planning to find summer jobs and maybe spend a few weeks climbing mountains in Washington or Alaska. But Marian?

All spring they had debated about summer camp for Marian but had put off any decision for so long that the best camps would no longer have any openings.

"We should have resolved this earlier," Evelyn complained.

"We did," Robert reminded her. "I suggested in January we register Marian for music camp at Cazadero but you didn't like the idea."

"There's that..."

Robert completed her sentence for her.

"...lake. Yes, there's that lake. Lake Cazadero. Ev, sooner or later, and it's bound to be sooner, as in three or four years and most likely two, she's going to have to learn to swim. We're going to have to *let* her learn to swim. We live on the coast, we're perched on a cliff at the edge of the Pacific Ocean. We're near beaches where kids she knows will be swimming and having parties every summer night. Marian is tall, she's suntanned, and blond and blue-eyed. She's beautiful. And she can't swim. I mean we don't permit her to swim."

"I don't want my daughter being a beach bum or a surf bum," Evelyn said crisply.

"You know your daughter will never..."

"Robert, Marian's skin is too delicate. Remember the pain she had when she was sick and her skin had those blisters from sunburn? She refuses to protect herself so we have to protect her. I don't know how long it will be, but for now we have to protect her from herself."

"Evelyn, your daughter is almost thirteen. In two years she'll be in high school where swimming classes are compulsory.'

"We can..."

"We can't, won't, send Marian to a private school just to keep her out of a swimming pool. Why are you so frightened at the idea of your daughter going into the water, of your daughter knowing how to swim?"

"I'm not frightened, Robert," Evelyn said, with great difficulty, even perhaps, guiltily.

"Ev, do you remember when we were thinking about buying this house? Remember how hard it was to get you to say yes? And remember how worried you were about access to the cliff and the beach? We solved the problem. We built that fence. What did it cost? Almost three thousand bucks, if I remember correctly. So, OK, that fence will keep out the whole Russian army when they attack us. But wait a minute. I just realized something."

"What?"

"You weren't interested in that fence keeping enemies out—those beach bums and those surfers—you were interested in that fence keeping your daughter *in*. Away from the water."

"Not true."

Evelyn was concentrating hard on the pot she was scrubbing. "You shouldn't have put out that bowl of chips," she said. "Kathy's folks don't want her eating junk food."

Robert, behind her, wrapped her in his arms and laughed. "You are such a phony," he said. "The famous mathematician is really a basic arithmetic teacher who can't add two and two and get four. She keeps getting five."

Evelyn, who frequently ended a discussion with "I'm simply stating a fact," offered Robert those words now, but they were followed by, "I'd like a glass of wine. How about you?"

"Sure. Then we can clink our glasses together and change the subject."

Robert Conroy, a tall man with a mane of blond hair, had been described recently by a reviewer of his latest book, as looking a bit like a slightly cynical Viking.

Now, at the once-again well-ordered table, the slightly cynical Viking reminded his wife she wasn't fooling him. She had tried to derail their discussion and failed.

"I want to remind you of some details," he said. "Some *facts*. Answer, please. Who was it who loved the view of the ocean from our cliff? Who stood there the first day we came here and stood on the cliff and took four thousand deep breaths and said how much she—she, mind you—loved the smell of the ocean? Who stands on the balcony outside our bedroom every night..."

"...not every night."

"...listening to the surf? Answer, please. I'll give you a hint. Female, initials Evelyn Conroy."

Evelyn accepted this good-naturedly but seemed uneasy. "That's two hints. You can't count. You were an English major. It's really the old love-hate thing, I guess."

"Love what and hate what?"

"Love the ocean, hate the ocean. The first day we saw this place I thought, and I said it to you, how easy it would be for our kids to sneak out and get down to that wild surf."

"Not kids. Kid. Singular. We only had Tommy at the time. He was two years old."

"Not quite two. I knew the odds favored the next child being a girl. One out of two. Fifty fifty. Those were the odds."

"Wait a minute." And Robert tilted his wife's chin up and grinned at her. "I just realized. It wasn't Todd you were worried about. You were worried about our having a girl. By George, I think I've got it. Evelyn Conroy is a sexist. Wait till I spread the news. It's OK for boys to crawl over fences and sneak around beaches but not girls. Girls can't be trusted."

Evelyn turned away.

Robert laughed. "Evelyn Conroy's a sexist," he chanted. "Evelyn Conroy's a sexist."

He stopped his joking when he saw his beloved wife drop her head into her arms.

Marian sat in the bleachers at the side of the pool, trying to be interested in the exchange between Kathy and her coach, or rather in the voice of the coach trying to motivate Kathy to do better. Five other observers were scattered in the bleachers.

As Kathy swam in Lane 1, the coach stomped along the edge of the pool, counting, shouting advice, checking his stopwatch, shouting more advice. Kathy never altered her stroke pattern but she did increase or decrease the beat of her legs as ordered.

The coach, still not satisfied, decided that simply by raising his voice he could get Kathy to try harder. "...your face comes out of the water too far when you roll your head to breathe...your rhythm's off...you have to concentrate..."

He counted aloud until Kathy reached the end of the pool and he continued counting after she left the water as if pulling her body out of the pool also had to be done by the numbers.

Marian restrained her impulse to amble down to the pool from the bleachers and nonchalantly stuff the swimsuit Kathy had loaned her into the mouth of the gesticulating and still-shouting coach. The bald, crimson-nosed tyrant was treating Kathy as he might treat a student learning to drive a car: "This is the brake, the brake stops the car, this is the gas pedal, the pedal sends gasoline to the engine..."

Kathy wasn't a machine and swimming for her wasn't an accumulation of numbered leg-beats or shaped-arm movements to be consciously or unconsciously synchronized with face-rolls. Swimming through water was like walking through air; you did it without premeditation, you enjoyed it because of the way water felt and smelled and tasted when it accepted you.

To escape the coach's voice, Marian got up and searched for the shower room, found it, located a locker and changed into the red suit Kathy had loaned her. It was tight but it would have to do. She was tempted for a moment to remove it, to go into the pool wearing nothing. That was how the body should be in the water: naked, unconfined by the restrictions of even the thinnest of thinnest cloth. But there were rules. And being a human meant you obeyed those rules even if you didn't respect them.

Pulling at the edges of the too-tight red cotton swimsuit that bit into her, Marian strolled back out to the pool and simply dropped, into the water.

Ahhh...

The classmates who had been scattered in the bleachers were gone now. The coach, somewhat subdued, was talking to Kathy in a softer but still grating voice. Marian, even under the water, could hear him say something to Kathy that was probably meant to be instructive. Still under water but gazing up toward the electrified ceiling of the pool-house, Marian saw the coach striding toward the locker room, passing over her without noticing her down in what could only be called heaven.

Marian rose and glided the length of the pool to where Kathy was sitting, head down, hands clenched between her legs, dangling her feet in the water. Kathy glanced absently at the pool, unaware that Marian Conroy not just in the water but *swimming* in the water.

Marian was swimming.

Marian Conroy was swimming quite leisurely as if she had been a swimmer in pools since birth.

"He said I don't want to be a champion, Mare. He said I don't want to work. He said he doesn't know why he's being paid to waste his time and my time. I said Mom and Dad want me to do this. That's why I'm here and that's why he's here. He's always yelling."

Then Kathy realized that she was gazing down at Marian and speaking to her in the water...in the water!

"Don't be scared, don't panic, Mare. I'm coming in. I'll teach you to float. Don't be scared. I'm a lifeguard, if you drown I'll save you."

Before Kathy could act, Marian lept leaped out of the water and onto the tile like a slithering eel, where she sat for a moment before she lowered herself over the edge of the pool and back into the water.

She continued descending, feet first, so conscious of the change from tile to water, so ecstatic in the descent through water that she wondered, even while descending, if she might just stay here forever inhaling water instead of air.

No, not here, not this water.

The smell and the taste of this water wasn't the smell or taste of ocean, this water tasted and smelled like the stuff she used to clean the bathrooms at home.

But this was water, this wasn't air.

And look at me, I am not walking, I am swimming.

Marian was swimming in fact with such smooth efficiency and speed that the coach, returned to retrieve his forgotten clipboard, started to offer some last-minute advice, thinking the body in the pool belonged to his lazy, unmotivated student. Bent over, fingers on the clipboard, the coach stopped talking when he realized that his lazy, unmotivated student was still sitting at the far end of the pool where he'd left her.

"Who the hell is that in the pool?"

Kathy tried to explain who her friend was and why she had brought her here to what was supposed to have been a private coaching session but, still in shock at the sight of Marian speeding through the water, she couldn't produce a sound.

Marian was in the pool.

Marian was swimming.

Marian was...

Marian Conroy was up from the bottom and not just rushing through the water with no splash, she was *speeding* through the water, she was maneuvering arms and legs and head with such grace and efficiency that Kathy and the now-awed coach could only watch in shocked silence.

Finally Kathy stood and pulled off her rubber cap. "Marian Conroy's my neighbor. My friend. I invited her. I'll pay the guest-fee, I promise."

The coach checked his watch. Or tried to.

He must have left his watch somewhere when he'd rushed back to retrieve his clipboard.

"She's been under for three minutes. She's just down there...on the bottom…as if she's sleeping. Get that girl out here. I want to talk to her."

Kathy waved her arms in a frantic effort to catch Marian's attention, to urge her to come up to the surface.

But with feet and hands faintly fluttering, indicating not just contentment but joy, Marian continued lying at the bottom of the pool.

Four minutes…five…six…

"She'll drown," the coach said. "I'll be sued." And he dove, fully clothed, into the water, intending to bring the probably now-lifeless body to the surface.

At that moment Marian shot up from the bottom with such force that she rose clear of the water's surface and, while still in the air, curved her body to dive again—head down, chin tucked in, arms out, hands clasped to return to the water and laughing.

The outraged coach tried to catch and hold her, but she slid through his arms and was out of the pool beside Kathy before the gasping coach realized he had been outmaneuvered and was embracing empty space.

Marian, like a preening seal, sat beside Kathy. She grinned, a modest, innocent, water-coated imp. "Don't you just love water, Kathy?"

The coach, hauling himself like a sick old monster out of the water and standing there dripping water onto his clipboard, said, "Who's your coach?"

≈

On the deck, Evelyn and Robert were having predinner martinis. Evelyn said, "I've been thinking about the music camp at Cazadero."

Robert sipped, clucked his tongue. "Too late. No more room. I checked. Anyway, there's something else we have to think about. I don't know quite how to tell you this." He took another sip, longer this time. "I had a call today from someone named Bruce Hamilton."

"Am I supposed to know a Bruce Hamilton?"

"He's the swimming coach at San Francisco Swimming Palace. He's coached three individual-swimmer winners for the Olympics and two gold medal teams. The Lumleys hired him to coach Kathy. Apparently Kathy's an Olympics-class swimmer."

"I didn't know that," Evelyn said.

"Bruce Hamilton said, and I quote, 'Marian Conroy is the finest swimmer I've ever seen in either the amateur or professional world since I've been a coach.' Bruce Hamilton also said, and I quote, 'If your daughter starts training now, meaning now, she could represent the United States in the Olympics in every category except perhaps diving and bring home as many as eight gold medals.' Unquote. His precise words."

Evelyn's face had turned a pale shade of gray. She seemed to shrink down into her chair, as if waiting to receive a fatal blow. "Where'd Bruce Hamilton see Marian Conroy swim? She's never taken lessons, she's never been in a pool. If Kathy Lumley has been secretly enticing Marian..."

Robert went on. "Marian visited Kathy at the high school pool when Kathy was having a session with the coach. Your daughter went into the water and swam, to quote the famous Bruce Hamilton again, 'like a fish'."

Evelyn pushed her hair away from her face, and Robert could see that her eyes were closed. She was having difficulty swallowing. "She disobeyed me. She's not to go in the water, in any pool, ever unless..."

"*Ever unless*, Ev? *Ever?* Marian's no longer a small child."

"She's my daughter. I don't want the world watching Marian win medals for swimming. Marian is going to lead a normal life. How about the boys? Are they Olympics material?"

"You don't mind the boys not leading a normal life? No, they're not Olympics material unless there's a new contest in beer-drinking and video-watching. So you say no to Marian working with Hamilton this summer?"

"A resounding *no!* In fact, I'm damn angry that Marian disobeyed me. That young lady is going to receive a lecture about trust and discipline."

But Robert believed that Evelyn seemed more sad than angry, as if, had she had the choice, she would rather have not known about her daughter's talent.

"Marian knows she isn't to go into pools, Ev. But we better be prepared, you and I both. She can't help herself. She can't live so close to the ocean without sooner or later, and I'm guessing sooner, wanting to wade into the ocean. And swim in the ocean."

"We'll move before that can happen."

"Wait a minute. We will not move before or after that can happen. Tell me, Ev. What if Marian wants to be a swimmer? What if—as you have a talent for math and I, apparently, have some talent for writing, and our sons have talent for something we'll discover a name for some day— what if our daughter has a talent for swimming? What if when she's twenty or so, she hates us for never having let her swim anywhere, pool or river or lake or ocean? Which, incidentally, is less than five hundred yards from her bedroom."

Evelyn took a long sip of her martini. She was trying to get back the anger of a moment before, trying to give it new life. "I want Marian to live a normal life, Robert. If she's furious when she's twenty, well, that's the chance we take as parents. We'll deal with it then. Marian doesn't need the attention that comes with winning a gold medal at the Olympics. She had enough attention when she was a baby and then a few years and then a couple of months ago to convince me that...."

"Oh," Robert said. "That. That was more than a couple months ago, professor."

Evelyn examined her hands. "In another year or two her fingers and toes will be clear."

Robert fingered his blond mustache. "She could have inherited my mustache. Be grateful for small favors. Ev, sweetheart, I'm gonna hang tough here."

"What's that mean?"

"We aren't going to move and you know we're not. We both make decisions about Marian, not one of us. I want Marian to take swimming lessons. In a few years she'll be going to beach parties with other kids and they'll be dancing and building bonfires and barbecuing and they'll be swimming in the ocean. As they ought to be doing. That's what California kids do, Ev. I don't know why you're so stubborn about this. Usually we talk and we make compromises and eventually things work out but on this one, talk doesn't get us anywhere. And I always yield. This time I'm going to hang tough."

"Hang tough? Come on, Robert. Speak grown-up lingo. You're not a teenager; you're an adult, you're a father."

"I'm *the* father here. As *the* father here, I want Marian to take swimming lessons this summer. If not from Hamilton, from someone."

For a moment Evelyn appeared to be on the verge of resistance, then, as she exhaled, her body seemed to deflate. "Well, what can I say? What can I do? I've been waiting for this. I guess I should be grateful you're taking the macho role on this one. I guess I've been hoping you would take the macho role eventually. OK. Will you work out the logistics? I know I'd just, well, to use a scientific term, I'd just go bonkers."

"My God, that was almost too easy. Am I going to have to pay big-time for this? Like take you to dinner at Chez Panisse or finally get that Tiffany lamp you've been dreaming about for two hundred years?"

At this point, staggering under a load of laughter, Marian led Kathy Lumley in through the front door. "Four more days of school," Marian shouted, rushing through the living room and out onto the patio. "Can Kathy and me have a sip of your martini to celebrate?"

"Kathy and I," Robert said.

"Oh, you too? Can Kathy and I and you and me have…?"

"Your mom and I are drinking adult drinks and having an adult conversation. You and Kathy can take some sodas to your room and…"

"Kathy," Evelyn said. "I won't tell your parents that in the kitchen, under the sink, in the second drawer, there's a big bag of your favorite gourmet potato chips. I won't tell your parents that no one in our family ever eats the blue chips but they always somehow disappear when I buy them. Don't get crumbs on the bed, please."

〜

Kathy fell onto Marian's bed. Marian, at the window, gazed down across the yard and the cliff to the ocean below. She came back to flop onto the bed beside Kathy.

"I have the feeling," Marian said, "this might be an interesting summer." She pulled her bare feet up. Taking one chip, she crunched it, made a face as if she might choke and dropped onto her back.

Kathy reached out to pull Marian's feet into the open, to touch the thin, barely visible, webbing between the toes.

"What's it feel like when I do that?" Kathy asked. "Does it feel like, I don't know, like extra stuff?"

"It feels like you're touching me."

"I've never looked real close at your hands, Mare. Can I?"

Marian extended both hands and Kathy ran her fingertips over the almost transparent pads where extra flesh had collected since her long-ago surgery. "You're never embarrassed," Kathy said, leaning forward for closer observation. "If it was me I'd think people are staring at me, I'd keep my hands in my pockets all the time. I'd probably wear gloves. I'd never take off my socks."

"I was born this way so I never think about it. Sometimes some kid in gym might make a joke but who cares? Mary Jo McKissick, you ever see her feet? Her toes are short and flat with almost no toenails. She gets more jokes than I do. And Roberta Jamison told me once, when she saw these scars from the surgery and we talked, she told me she has so much hair all over her body she has to go to a doctor's office every three months to have it peeled off. Not peeled but...I don't know...shaved or something."

Kathy said June Miller had problems too. "June's boobs are so big her folks spend lots of money on medicines to keep them from getting bigger. She's thirteen and the guys tease her. She's absent so much she's failing all her classes. And she's really smart."

"Being smart doesn't help or hurt. You're the way you are, that's all. It's no one's fault." She stretched forward to touch her bare toes. "My Grandma Audrey had it. Syn...syndac-ta-ly. This. This webbing."

Kathy widened her eyes, pretending to be impressed.

"I've practiced the word recently," Marian said. "That's what it's called, when you're born with webbed skin between your fingers and toes. Syndactyly."

Kathy, fascinated, said, "Yeah, you told me. It's in your family. How far back does it go?"

"Grandma Audrey had it and her grandmother had it. And that grandmother's grandmother. It's almost always sent down through the women and it usually skips a generation. That's probably why Mom never had it. Grandma told me all this...we talk about it secretly, because Mom doesn't like to talk about it, to me or anyone...Grandma Audrey told me Mom worries about me having it."

"Your grandma's grandma's grandma?"

"Maybe even farther."

"It can't, Mare. That would be before Abraham Lincoln. Before George Washington, even. I bet that's even before Jesus Christ."

Marian shrugged, superior in her possession of such secret information. "It goes back to before human beings lived on this earth."

They both said, "Grandma Audrey told me that," and they both laughed.

Then they stared at each other, trying to comprehend the implications. It was uncomfortable to think of time being endless and of normal life being so random.

Marian thought about something else, something she couldn't even tell Kathy, something else she had difficulty even thinking about.

Those conversations, those secret exchanges with Grandma Audrey: had they actually happened?

She tried to remember where and when her grandmother had told her about such traits existing in the distant past, when humans hadn't yet arrived on this earth, when creatures like dinosaurs crawled through the marshes and fish possessed legs that permitted them to survive on land as well as in the ocean.

Had those details been disclosed during one visit? Several visits? Several secret private conversations?

Had she known all this before she was born?

Had her grandmother told her? And had she forgotten?

"Kathy, what do they call a baby when it's not born yet? When it's still inside its mother? I forget."

"Is this a trick question? This is a puzzle, right? If I get the right answer I get a prize?"

"Fetus. I remembered."

"Not fair. You didn't give me a chance."

Marian said slowly, "Mom and Dad went to college and Todd and Tommy are in college now and Mom's a professor and a mathematician and Dad's a writer and no one, not one of them, ever talks about what I want to talk about."

"You mean boys? You mean what's-her-name who got her nose pierced?"

"This."

"Your toes and fingers?"

"My toes and fingers."

From the kitchen Evelyn Conroy announced they were going to a movie. "You guys want to go with us? Kathy, you want to call home and ask your folks? We won't, definitely won't, well—maybe we won't, should we—stop afterwards at Lyn's Hot Dogs for Hepcats."

Marian, whooping, led Kathy down the hallway.

Every coach in every high school in California had heard about the swimming prowess of Marian Conroy and had written letters, sent e-mails, telephoned, rung the doorbell, prayed.

But Evelyn's rules remained in force.

Marian Conroy, she and Robert agreed, would not become the property of ambitious coaches who sell athletes the way other hucksters peddle cars and refrigerators.

But as determined (Robert sometimes used the word *obsessed*) as Evelyn Conroy continued to be, she also was slowly becoming aware of some very important things. Aware, first, that a mathematics professor might be able to calculate time but not control it. Nor its consequences.

And aware, second, that Marian Conroy was no longer a child to be protected. Marian would very soon, too soon, be...was already...a teenager.

And aware that Marian—next week, next month, next year (if she weren't already)—would be spending time not just with Kathy Lumley but with other teenagers, a category that included *boys*.

Boys.

"Robert, do you think Marian can be trusted to protect herself?"

"Why do you ask? You think she ought to take karate classes?"

"I'm serious, Robert. We've never kept secrets from her about the risks out there..."

"We haven't?"

"She's a beautiful young woman, Robert. Boys..."

"Oh, that. I mean them. Boys. Men. Guys."

Marian wasn't just attractive, she was beautiful, as Kathy kept reminding everyone.

Kathy had said, "Mrs. Conroy..."

"Evelyn. It's time you call me Evelyn. I've been calling you Kathy for years. Does Marian call your parents *Mr.* Lumley or *Mrs.* Lumley?"

"She calls them Angela and Frank. Well, she calls my mother Angela and my father Frank."

"I'm so glad she can distinguish one from the other. To you, Kathy, from this day on, I am Evelyn."

Kathy said, "Evelyn, I bet Marian could be Miss California if she wanted to. She could be Miss America if she wanted to. She could be in the Olympics if she wanted. My coach..."

When Evelyn reported the conversation to Robert, he chuckled. But Evelyn found Kathy's remarks a little uncomfortable.

Both Conroys reminded each other almost daily, almost hourly, that in another year or two Marian would be going out on dates unchaperoned.

Evelyn wondered now and then (though she hadn't discussed this with Robert) if Marian might already be meeting boys on those long Saturday afternoons when she and Kathy were supposed to be at the mall or biking along the coast.

Evelyn knew, without Robert reminding her, that this year or next year Marian would be going to and occasionally giving beach parties.

Beach parties.

Beach.

Sand and shore.

Breakers.

Waves.

Ocean.

For as long as she could, Evelyn Conroy was determined to have a hand and a voice in charting her daughter's course through adolescence.

Considered something of a control-freak by other members of Berkeley's Math Department, Professor Conroy, might not be able to delay her daughter's growing up but she could carefully control her introduction to the world of the adolescent.

"I will determine Marian's childhood. I, me, Evelyn Conroy, not

Hollywood."

"We," Robert said. "We, Robert and Evelyn Conroy, we will de…"

"When I say 'I' I mean 'we'."

"Yeah, sure, Professor. And when I write a plus-sign in my checkbook I mean it to mean minus."

≈

Two days after the school year ended, Evelyn and Robert went with Marian through the gate and down the path that skirted the cliff and onto the beach. "The whole nine yards," Evelyn said, setting up an umbrella and laying out blankets and towels and ice chests and distributing tubes of sunscreen.

For the occasion, Evelyn had even bought a new bathing suit for herself.

Robert wore cut-offs and huarache sandals from Mexico.

Marian?

The day before, Marian, with her mother's consent, had spent two hours with Kathy at Wet Seal, in downtown San Francisco. After almost two hours trying on suits, she had finally submitted to the pleas of both Kathy and the young sales clerk. She bought a two-piece tankini.

"Shows a little cleavage," the clerk said. "Not too much, just enough."

"Enough for what?" Marian asked.

"And belly button," Kathy whispered, wide-eyed, "It shows your belly button. I love the color. Of the suit, not the belly button."

"That's called color-blocking," the clerk said. "Different shades of different colors depending on how you're hit by the sun and shade."

"Mom will freak."

At the beach, Mom did freak when Marian, at the beach threw off her robe and stood, tall and slim with blue eyes flashing and long blond hair flying in the wind.

Mom tried not to stare but failed. She also gasped while trying not to gasp. Hoping to say something suitably parental, she ended up with, "Oh, Marian, I love it. Robert, look at her. She's gorgeous!"

Kathy and Marian struck high-tens and high-twenties.

The Conroy family and Kathy relaxed on the sand together, reading to each other, playing cards together. Evelyn tried to teach them all the basics of bridge.

Marian was an expert within minutes.

Robert confessed he would never care for the game because of the terms significant at the bridge table. Dummy? Someone gets to be the dummy? Hey, the opportunity of a lifetime!

On their third afternoon at the beach, Evelyn and Marian and Kathy played bridge while Robert, reading print-out pages of his new manuscript, served as the perfect dummy.

Marian and Kathy couldn't stay out of the water but, aware of Evelyn's anxiety, they almost never wandered beyond the surf. When they did go farther they would look back and see Evelyn Conroy standing in the sand near her blanket, watching them through binoculars.

On the first Saturday in July, Evelyn and Robert were sitting on their blanket, protected by a huge red umbrella, when Evelyn interrupted her reading of a Ph.D. thesis and jumped up. She'd distinctly heard Kathy Lumley calling, "Mare, come back. Come back, Mare."

Dropping the bound thesis and running toward the surf, Evelyn saw Kathy standing almost up to her hips in the surf, her hands cupped to her mouth, shouting "Mare, come back."

As she ran, Evelyn saw Marian far out at sea, swimming parallel to the shore. Parallel, thank God.

Evelyn ran across the sand and dove into the oncoming wave and swam harder and faster than she had when she had won her trophies for the Berkeley women's water polo team twenty years before.

Being a mathematician helped her reach Marian quickly. Without realizing she was using mathematical principles, her course—at that precise rate and angle through the water—brought her, after two minutes, about ten feet in front of her daughter. She could see a large gray-white fin that protruded above the water, following Marian's foaming wake.

Even as Evelyn identified the shape as a shark fin she saw Marian turn and swim away from the shore, toward the horizon. Evelyn saw the shark turn and she watched it follow, drawing closer and closer to her daughter.

Evelyn, screaming, kicked and stroked faster and harder.

Her sound and motion distracted the shark from its pursuit of Marian. It turned to take the screaming figure closest to it...Evelyn.

Even before the shark turned, Marian shot up above the water.

She heard the screaming as she saw the fin moving toward her mother. She lunged up out of the water to intercept the shark, and dropped her whole weight on the open-jawed shark head. Screaming, she beat and clawed with fists and feet and toenails and fingernails. Those screams were not the sounds of a frightened teenage girl but of a killer whale, an orca, moving to kill its natural enemy, the shark.

The water was a storm of foam as the shark, trying to attack and defend itself at the same time, was rapidly outmaneuvered by this new beast that was pounding its head and promising destruction.

The shark turned and swam, faster than before, away from the two humans, out to sea, toward the horizon.

Marian floated for a moment to regain breath and strength. When she turned and she saw her mother's face inches from her own, she tried to bring herself back from that state of shocked bliss that had possessed her.

"Mom!"

And she felt her mother's arms around her.

"Mom...mom."

"Come on darling. Let's go back. It's gone."

"Where are we?"

"We're out here in the water, in the ocean."

"How'd we...how'd you get here?"

"I swam. But I have to get back, baby. My stamina isn't what it used to be. Neither...neither is...anything else."

"I'm...I don't think I can make it. I didn't know...I'm tired, Mom."

Evelyn Conroy didn't have to use all of her long-forgotten experience as a summer lifeguard but she did select pieces of it...urging herself to remain calm, reassuring the victim, positioning the victim, placing her cupped hand under the victim's chin, stroking with one arm along with the beat of her legs, pulling her victim toward shore.

Marian didn't resist. Closing her eyes, she could believe that this had all been carefully planned were it not for the shark. And she had saved her mother.

"I love you, Mom."

That afternoon Evelyn, having commandeered Robert's woolen robe and consumed her eighth cup of hot tea, said to her husband, "I'm glad she was swimming parallel to the shore. If she'd been heading out to sea I'd never have caught her. Her stroke and kick puts me to shame."

Robert had almost kneeled and prayed on that beach.

When his wife had crawled back through the surf, their daughter in her arms, he and Kathy had grabbed and dragged them farther up onto the beach. By the time a crowd and lifeguard had arrived, the Conroys and Kathy were safely back home.

He didn't say now, as he was tempted, "Well, that's one problem solved."

Nor, later that evening, after Marian and Kathy had left the dinner table and gone to Marian's room, did he say, "Well, that's one problem solved." He did say, "You're a courageous woman, Ev. I've loved you for almost 30 years so I knew you were smart. But I never knew you were so courageous."

"I'm a realist," she said. "That's why I'm a mathematician. Or maybe it's the other way around."

"I admire realistic fiction."

"Fiction is fantasy," said Evelyn smiling to divert any possible argument. "In fiction the writer decides what he—or she—decides is true. In science certain things simply *are* true. Period. Exclamation point."

In Marian's bedroom, Kathy, sat at the foot of the bed and stared at her friend's face."I was sure you were dead," Kathy said, her voice hoarse. "And I was sure your mom was dead. Then you..."

"I what?"

"Marian Conroy, I hate you. You did what you did and you pretend it was nothing. You turned that shark around and you had him tumbling over himself so many times he tied himself in a knot."

Marian, after considering this, said, "It was a she."

"What?"

"That shark was a she. A her."

A few weeks later, during the first week of August, the dense fog was a constant presence along the coast, so filled with moisture it might as well have been rain.

Evelyn woke up one night to the sound of intense coughing coming from Marian's room. She went into her daughter's room to find her kneeling on the floor, leaning forward onto the bed. The sheet and blanket were lying in a heap on the floor. Her body was glossy with perspiration.

Evelyn returned Marian to bed, covered her with a blanket, and woke Robert, who called Ted Longacre.

Ten minutes later Dr. Longacre, in robe and slippers, his black bag on the floor at his feet, was sitting on Marian's bed.

Marian opened her eyes and saw Ted sitting there, stethoscope around his neck. Her mother and father were behind Ted, both of them looking frightened.

Ted's voice was very serious. "So, Mare, you got the nasties again. Well, I have to poke around and I have to ask some questions. Can you tell me what's going on? Inside your tum, I mean?"

As she described the sore throat, the nausea, and the heavy fatigue, Marian endured the poking and thumping of fingers on chest and back, the press of the stethoscope, the cough-on-commands.

"Anything else, Mare?"

"My legs ache."

She tried to describe the pains, tried to locate them, but it seemed that, even as she talked, the pains were suddenly no longer restricted to her calves or her thighs. Both hips hurt so much she wanted to cry.

"Where? Here?"

"There, yes. Both hips."

After the probings and the questions and the responses Ted kissed Marian on the forehead and said he was going to give her some pills that would both relax her and take the pain away. Then he turned to Evelyn and Robert. "I want Marian in the hospital."

"When?" Robert asked.

"Now."

Marian sounded alarmed. "Now? This minute?"

"I'll call the hospital to prepare. But yes, *now*. I want you to have some tests that can only be done at the hospital. You'll stay overnight.

49

Maybe even stay more nights. We'll know more after we get the test results."

But Marian was already dropping off to sleep.

$$\approx$$

Sitting in the Conroys' living room. Ted Longacre was now dressed and ready for the 20-minute drive to the hospital.

When Evelyn returned from Marian's bedroom, carrying a suitcase of essentials, Ted said, "I've called Admissions. They're ready. I'll drive. You're both too upset to drive."

"That would be wise," Robert said. Evelyn nodded in agreement.

"But let's talk for a minute before we leave," Ted said. "While you were getting ready I made myself some coffee. You might like a cup. It could help you relax while you hear me out. "The scenario might be predicted with fair certainty."

Twice having found fluid in Marian's lungs, Ted Longacre was tempted to keep Marian in the hospital for more than a day or two. The best endocrinologist in the country was in San Francisco this week. Ted knew him well, they had been classmates at Yale. He wanted to examine Marian himself this evening and perhaps give her several of his own tests.

"I'm not a gambling man," Ted said, "but I'd bet tonight and tomorrow's tests will show what we found the last two times will happen this time. With symptoms that suggestive of serious, possibly fatal, illness in most people, instead, Marian will be swimming at the beach again in three or four days."

"But?" Evelyn said.

"But I'm concerned about something else. What if this illness keeps recurring every five or six or seven years? Or every eight or nine years? It's more serious this time than it was the last time. Will it become even more serious the next time? Perhaps most important, what's its source? What precautions or medications are possible? Is it, can it be, fatal?"

Evelyn and Robert grabbed for each other's hands.

"I didn't tell you," Ted said, "what I did after our first session and, again, after our last session. I'll tell you now. I was much more concerned than I let on. I sent the results of all tests from both events to four different research centers. The last time, people at all four centers predicted Marian would be dead in four days. By the time I received those reports Marian had recovered and was racing Kathy Lumley up and down the sidewalk. I can't say that we'll be as fortunate...that Marian will be as fortunate...this time. Or every time."

"Is this going to be the story of Marian's life?" Robert Conroy asked. "Is there a chance she might not recover? Is there someone we can go to who knows more about this—who knows what works and what doesn't, what causes it and what doesn't?"

"We'll have to explore all that," Ted said.

As Robert collected the cups and carried them into the kitchen he heard Evelyn ask, "Is there anything in medical literature that relates to her problem?"

"Nothing," Ted said. "There's not a shred of documented history in the library or on the Internet. Given the bizarre nature of many childhood diseases and their disappearance with the onset of hormonal maturity, Marian could possibly outlive all her peers. At the age of eighty or ninety Marian might still be having these strange attacks. She might go on to celebrate her hundredth birthday. Chances are, however..."

"Chance," Evelyn Conroy said, "isn't in my vocabulary."

"OK," Ted said. "Let's get Marian and be on our way. Do you want me to...?"

"I'll carry her," Robert said.

6

Six physicians, all of them specialists, visited Marian at the hospital that night and the next day. Marian gave up trying to remember their names except for one that she couldn't forget. McLaughlin.

"Dr. Ellsworth McLaughlin is a specialist from Johns Hopkins," Ted told Marian when he introduced them. "Marian is my almost-daughter, Ellsworth. I brought her into the world."

An hour before, when Ted introduced Dr. McLaughlin to Evelyn and Robert Conroy, the doctor expressed his skepticism, saying it must be a joke. He'd read all the reports, all the letters and he'd heard Ted's description of the recoveries. There were too many improbabilities in this case.

Evelyn was about to refuse to let him into her daughter's room, when Ted said, "An eccentric, but the best thoracic surgeon in the world. Right, Ellsworth?"

Neither of the Conroys was convinced. Or impressed.

"Evelyn, Robert, Dr. McLaughlin is on the staff at Johns Hopkins and he was one of the experts I sent Marian's earlier reports to. He didn't know the reports concerned the same patient until now. He's giving a lecture at Stanford tonight and he's doing us a very great favor taking time to be here with Marian."

Neither Evelyn nor Robert appeared impressed yet, or mollified, but they yielded.

Dr. McLaughlin huffed and puffed at Marian's bedside, brusquely putting several questions to her. No, she couldn't recall any special warnings of the pain or the nausea. No, she couldn't remember being brought to the hospital. No, she didn't know what day it was or what month.

"Your temperature is very...very low. You don't feel weak now... you're not...your mind's not wandering? You appear alert. Are you trying to deceive us in some way? For some reason?"

"No, I know I'm in St. Paul's Hospital, I'm in Room 432, my doctor is that beautiful man standing there beside you and his name is Ted Longacre, the tall blonde Viking standing next to him is Robert Conroy, my dad, and the woman standing next to him is Evelyn Conroy, my gorgeous mother. And your name is...what's your name again?"

Dr. McLaughlin, without tempering his voice, asked Evelyn and Robert Conroy if their daughter had ever exhibited signs of mental instability.

"You mean am I nuts?" Marian asked, laughing.

Straining for decorum, Dr. McLaughlin examined Marian and jotted on a sheet of paper the various examinations to be performed. Then, after lifting Marian's right eyelid and her left eyelid and grunting to himself, he nodded to Marian's parents and started out of the room, stopped and returned to Marian's bedside.

Taking Marian's hand in his own, he said, "I will remember you all my life, young woman. You are the smartest and bravest and prettiest patient I have ever met. Some day you'll find it possible to indulge big ugly boars like me. A boar is just a big bear spelled incorrectly." After disappearing through the door, his growl of a voice called back, "You're fortunate parents, Mr. And Mrs. Conroy. Talk to you later, Ted."

"What a nice guy," Robert Conroy said.

⋙

At the end of the day, Ted and Dr. McLaughlin sat in an examining suite that contained on-wall illuminators covered with x-ray films and, posted on bulletin boards and taped to walls, ten or twelve charts. All the paraphernalia required for full and final analysis of every button pushed and every needle injected the previous twenty-four hours stood at the ready in this room.

Dr. McLaughlin leaned back in his chair, loosened his red tie, unbuttoned his collar, sighed, and said, "There is more fluid in this girl's lungs than I've seen in drowning victims that have been under water for five days. Her lungs aren't only significantly diminished in capacity compared to two years ago, the alveolae have altered in both shape and size and...I hesitate to say this...these are the lungs one might expect to find in a sea mammal. But note something here, Ted. Pictures of the lungs taken one hour ago indicate an ongoing alteration. I say ongoing because I'd wager tomorrow's films will show additional alteration."

Ted checked one sheet of figures against another, one set of films against another. "Am I correct? Are the lungs returning to the shape and size they were yesterday, when she came in?"

"You're correct. To be honest, nobody in any research institute in the world will believe our new and current report when we offer it. As I didn't believe you yesterday, I have to confess. If I weren't here, participating in the exam, I wouldn't believe a word of the history you'll be offering our associates. But I've met the patient. Now, consider these computer printouts from the six scans."

Ted leaned in close.

"Ted, if this were my patient I would insist on immediate tubing of the lungs. She must get rid of that fluid. I would have a thorough chemical analysis. What are the components of that fluid, or fluids, what is its source? Or their sources. These shadows here, these lumps of tissue? They could be tumors. These shadows here?" he said pointing. "Your radiologist supports my findings that the top of the thighbone is demineralized, meaning it's just simply melting away. On a fourteen- or fifteen-year-old? Impossible. Unless. These shadows right here could be metastasis. The child could be developing cancer, Ted. I say *could be*. Now here is where I can speak with authority. The lungs."

Ted leaned closer to have a clearer view of the films of Marian's lungs.

"If surgery isn't performed by tomorrow morning this patient could die by tomorrow evening. This isn't a prediction, Ted, this is a statement. A fact."

〰

Dr. Longacre had to tell Evelyn and Robert Conroy. And Marian.

Marian accepted the information so calmly that Ted thought she might not have heard him.

Evelyn and Robert, both in tears, reminded Marian that Dr. McLaughlin was the best lung specialist in the country and if he recommended surgery she should...

"No."

Marian's refusal was so immediate, so sharp, so emphatic, that the adults in the room were shaken.

"I know I'm not a grown-up but you have to trust me. I'm going to get better very very fast."

Evelyn dropped to her knees at the side of the bed. "You don't understand, Marian."

"I do understand, Mom."

Robert tried to reason with Marian. When she was older, when she had more experience, she would have her rights, but she was a minor now, and they, her father and mother, her parents, would have to make decisions for her. "We *have to*, baby."

"I can't stop you, Dad. But all that stuff Dr. McLaughlin wants to do won't help. Please don't let him cut me open. If he does I'll die right here in this hospital. I know it. If he doesn't, I'll live."

Dr. Longacre held Marian's hand. "How about we wait two hours?"

"How about ten hours?"

"Eight hours. If you're not showing dramatic improvement in eight hours..."

"If I'm not better in eight hours you can cut me open. But if I'm showing improvement I get to go home."

Dr. Ellsworth McLaughlin was on a plane en route to New York the next morning when Marian sat up in her hospital bed for two cups of green tea and three slices of buttered toast.

"God works in mysterious ways," Ted Longacre told the Conroys. "All signs are positive. Marian is so improved it's absolutely scary."

"Her lungs," Evelyn said.

"I'll repeat what Ellsworth McLaughlan said when his driver picked him up. 'Regarding Marian Conroy. I can't decide whether I should spank the child or tour with her as a creature of heavenly inspiration. I've always believed that God didn't create humans to live underwater. Fish, yes, humans, no. Would her recovery prove the existence of miracles? If I remember correctly—I might have missed it—but miracles weren't in the curriculum at Yale Med.'"

"Well, should we still be concerned?" Evelyn asked.

"Yes. At least until we, meaning everyone I've brought into this, comes up with either an explanation or a resolution. Weaving in and out of all the responses from all the scientists who have gotten back to me is the expectation that as Marian matures, this mystery could fade away. By the time Marian has finished maturing and has children of her own, science will be more advanced and, I hope, will simply shrug off our exasperation."

"I hope," Evelyn said, "she has only boys."

Ted Longacre slapped his head. "I am stupid."

Evelyn Conroy waited.

"We never thought to have Todd and Tommy examined. Evelyn, we have to do that."

Evelyn was so positive when she said, "You won't find anything helpful," Robert laughed.

"How do you know, Ev?" he asked, smiling. "I think you and I ought to be examined too."

"Yes," Ted Longacre said. "Absolutely."

"Examined for what? Fluid in the lungs? The only fluid you'll find in my lungs is Westmar's Pinot Noir '98. No, thanks. No physical for me."

Behind his wife's back Robert Conroy signaled to Ted Longacre to back off, to leave everything to him. He'd convince his wife.

〰

On Marian's first night out of the hospital, Tommy and Todd came home from college. They were waiting at the house when Robert's car appeared and gathered at the passenger's door to help their sister into the house. They ended up racing her to see who could make it to the porch first. She won.

Todd put off cramming for a French test, saying, "I'll tell you the truth. I'd rather fail French than miss out on being near my baby sister."

Tommy put thumb and forefinger, a pretend pistol, to his brother's temple.

"Baby?" Marian sneered.

After a quick meal, the whole family gathered in Marian's bedroom to watch a Harry Potter video that Evelyn and Robert called first-grade-ish and Marian and the boys agreed wasn't so much first-grade-ish as kindergarten-ish.

That night, after the boys had gone to bed and Robert was snoring lightly, Evelyn left her bed and tiptoed into Marian's room.

Marian was on her back, sleeping, appearing healthy, almost angelic.

Evelyn didn't know that though her daughter's eyes were closed and her breathing heavy, she was wide awake.

When her mother left the room Marian opened her eyes and stared into the darkness. Then she rose, slid open the door, stood on the deck listening to the roar of the surf far below and inhaling the scent of the sea. She knew that for the moment she didn't have voice enough to return the calls spilling out of the depths of the ocean far to the west.

She crossed the patio and descended through the terraced beds of shrubs. She climbed the fence, dropped onto the path beyond and hurried down the hillside to the shore where she threw off her nightgown and ran forward through the surf into the oncoming wave. With a movement that was part-breaststroke, part-crawl, with sinuous undulations of legs that began at her hips and traveled to her feet and toes, she moved toward the invisible horizon.

Earth no longer existed.

Mother, father, brothers, Kathy no longer existed.

All that existed was the rise and the fall of loving water that contained songs and whispers. Song whispers. Whispered songs.

Then they found her. They approached with almost chiding calls and whistles and clicks. Where have you been? Why have you stayed away so long? We needed you. There were others like you. They needed you.

Others like her? Humans like her? Those humans needed her?

The sleek silken bodies pressed close, sending their voices into and through her skin, ribs, lungs, and into her brain.

First one and then another—some as small as her hand, some larger than the house on that far away cliff—one and then another came close to slide over and under and against her body, her face, her fingers. She yearned to talk to them, to communicate her love for them as they were communicating their love for her. Did they know that soo she would be telling them that they were brothers and sisters, mother and father?

Then, acting apparently by some pre-arrangement, singly and in pairs, they nudged and carried and guided her back toward shore.

Not yet, she heard. Over and over. *Not yet. Before...you could have helped before...those others such as you...*

And then she heard another...*soon...soon.*

And again...*soon.*

And, in the deep dark distance, the human voices calling to her, pleading with her...calling...pleading...

〰

Marian returned along the hillside path, carrying her nightgown.

In the shower, face turned up, eyes closed against the spray, Marian heard her mother in her room, calling, "Marian! Marian!"

Marian turned off the shower and opened the curtain.

"Marian, what in heaven's name are you doing taking a shower at four o'clock in the morning?"

"I woke up, Mom. I feel fine. I just woke up and wanted a shower."

"You're wearing your nightgown."

"Sure. Now it doesn't have to be washed."

For just a fraction of a second, Evelyn Conroy remembered those words of Dr. McLaughlin. What were they? "Has the child ever been irrational?" No, that wasn't exactly it. But there had been something suggesting mental instability.

"Go back to bed, Mom. I am. As soon as I dry myself."

Evelyn twisted water from Marian's nightgown. "I'll put it in the dryer," she said. "You sure you're OK?"

"Want me to recite the multiplication tables? Want to know the square root of 144?"

"Oh, go to bed."

Evelyn turned off the light, wondering if she should go to campus today. Should she cancel her classes? Should she persuade Robert to stay home? Should she call Ted and arrange for that nurse?

"Is Kathy coming over today?," she asked. "Are you going to her house?"

"She's coming over and we're going to bike to the mall. We're going to shop. Just, I don't know, for whatever we see. We're going mall-malling. That's what Kathy calls it."

Nothing to worry about, Evelyn decided. She's as close to normal as a teen can be.

"What would you like for breakfast? Muffins?"

"You guys go on. I'll sleep in and make my own breakfast, Mom. I remember where the kitchen is."

Normal.

〜〜〜

When Marian got up and went into the kitchen, she sat where her mother had already laid out the bowl and the spoon and the napkin and the box of cereal.

The day's *San Francisco Chronicle* had been shoved to the side of the table. The front page contained a photograph of Coast Guard vessels at sea.

Ship Sinks Mile Off Coast. 14 Men Lost.

"The Irma Sanchez, a tanker registered under the flag of Liberia, sank off the coast of San Francisco at 2:06 this morning, after an explosion in the aft..."

Those others...

〜〜〜

Grandma Audrey phoned that night just as the Conroys finished dinner. For privacy, Marian went to her room. She heard the click when her mother hung up the phone in the dining room.

"I was going to call you this evening, Grandma."

"You and I are on the same wavelength, I guess. Anything special?"

"I was going to ask if I could visit you sooner than we planned. Not next summer or the summer after that but this summer."

"This summer's almost over, Marian. In a few weeks it will be fall. In fact the leaves are already beginning to turn. It's been cold. I should tell you...that wavelength again...I should tell you that I just asked your mother if you could visit me for a few days next week. She just couldn't manage it."

"Meaning she said no."

"Correct. She said, '*You* must visit us, Mother.' I must tell you, Marian. I'm a busy woman these days, getting things in order. I'm an old woman, you know. I hate to fly. And I'm too impatient to take a train. But we shall work it out. You will visit me here very soon. Let me speak to your mother, my dearest."

As Marian went to tell her mother that Grandma Audrey wanted to talk to her, she wondered why Grandma never, when referring to Evelyn, said *my daughter* or just plain *Evelyn*.

It was always *your mother*.

Days and nights followed days and nights, semesters chased semesters, the three years before Marian's senior year of high school passed so fast that Marian's periods of illnesses became nearly forgotten memories, "fig newtons of the imagination," as a character in one of Robert Conroy's books said.

Marian's senior year in high school began like the previous three, with the same appeals from college swimming coaches and recruiters. This year, her college-decision year, the meetings and e-mails and phone calls and letters all had an air of desperation.

" '*Bye-bye, happiness, bye-bye, everyone,*'" Kathy sang. "After this year, Mare, we'll be out there in the big wide world. Looking for jobs or going to college or both. You gonna' keep pretendin' you're just Miss Suzie from Suzeville, Mare? You could go to the best college in the world if you wanted to say so-take-me to one of those swim coaches."

"If I decide to go to college it's going to be wherever you go."

"Mare, we gotta stop meetin' like this. People'll begin to think we're man and wife."

"People'll think we're wife and wife. Couldn't care less."

"I can see it now. You come over to baby-sit my kids and I say, 'Hey, whatever you guys do, don't get in the water with this lady. It'll destroy your ego.' "

"Yo, man! The word is *self esteem.*"

College.

In the Lumley and the Conroy houses, the catalogues and letters to-

and-from were stacked knee high. What other choices were there? Marriage? Children?

At eighteen?

College decisions, as the year advanced, became more important than boys and parties and gossip, more serious than having fun.

Most of Marian's more scholarly friends were thinking and talking about college applications and the hierarchy of distinction, from Harvard to Oakland Tech. Many, like Marian and Kathy, were preoccupied with creating memories of that final summer of youth. For some, friendships that had developed into almost demented intimacies began to show fracture lines.

Marian and Kathy were more fortunate.

Together every possible minute of every possible hour, they relied on each other for sustenance, physical and emotional. Though dividing their time between their houses, Kathy didn't even try to conceal her favorite—the Conroy house, with its gourmet potato chips for the asking and Ben and Jerry's pistachio ice cream.

Evelyn and Robert Conroy had adapted to the loss of their sons to the outside world. Their unused rooms became repositories for accumulated junk. They were now preparing themselves for the departure of their daughter for college and anticipating the coming pleasures and pains of an empty nest.

Marian was still envied by every girl in the senior class, still chased by what Kathy called "the cutest studs in San Francisco." She was also still chased by coaches from at least fifty college swimming programs with offers of financial aid that could, Robert said, "pay for a hundred graduate students doing research for my books for the next ten years."

Academics? Marian Conroy was still the best student, the best debater, the best...At school and at parties, she heard the sometimes resentful mantra *you've got it made, Mare,* so often the words no longer registered.

Evelyn and Robert had long ago assured each other—and by now had just about convinced Ted Longacre—that those strange illnesses of the past were unlikely to ever occur again. And even if variations of those dark days should return, disaster was no longer possible.

Just last week *Sports Illustrated* wanted to publish a cover story about Marian Conroy (...*that not-once-in-a-decade but once-in-a-century athlete...*).

Marian's response when the phone call came was "Forget it."

Evelyn and Robert Conroy's response when the editor called again to speak to the parents: "She says forget it. When our daughter says *forget it* she means *forget it.*"

Ted Longacre maintained a continuing interest in his neighbor/friend/almost-daughter. He had kept his promise to the Conroys and to himself, and every four or five months he had examined Marian in his office or her home. He recorded her temperature, her patterns of headaches, her sudden unusual responses to certain foods, her miscellaneous aches and pains. In a drawer in his desk were two folders labeled *Marian Conroy*, each of them more than two inches thick.

If Dr. Longacre, who had become a minor celebrity in the medical-scientific world for his refusal to permit articles about Marian to be published in any journal, saw no dark clouds on or beyond the horizon, Evelyn and Robert figured there was no reason for them to fear approaching storms.

Late in November, at four in the afternoon, when Marian saw Ted's station wagon drive into their garage, she met him as he started up the steps to his back porch. Ted started to welcome her with a cheerful greeting when he paused. Why was his heart sinking?

"I'm sick," Marian said. "Mom and Dad haven't come home yet so..."

"Come inside," Ted said.

Pauline, Ted's wife, was in the kitchen, preparing dinner. She greeted Marian and then she, too, sensed something from the expression on Ted's face. "Would you like a cup of tea, Mare? I just made a pot of green tea for myself."

"Marian's not feeling well," Ted said. "Let's go to the living room, Mare. Now tell me about it."

Pauline accompanied them and sat on the sofa beside Marian, holding her hand while Marian considered what to say and how to say it.

"My legs," Marian said.

Ted waited.

"My legs hurt."

"The same pain you had before? In the same places?"

"I'm not sure. It's been so long I forget. I think it's different in a way, and it's in different places. Sort of deeper inside the muscles, almost as if it's in the center of the bones."

Ted waited. He knew by now that waiting for Marian to talk would produce more information than scattershot questions.

"I was doing splits. I've done them for years. One day, about a week ago, I could hardly spread my legs. Then today I fell. Twice. I didn't trip on anything, I just fell. I never fall. And I had a hard time getting up. My legs seemed to lock together."

"Do you have any pain now? Right now?"

"Hardly any right this minute."

"Anything else? Nausea? Sore throat? Headaches?"

"No. But, well, there is something else."

Pauline Longacre, still clutching Marian's hand, said, "Do you want me to leave, Mare?"

"No, no. Please stay. Mom and Dad will be home pretty soon but I want to talk to Ted first."

"Shall I call them and leave a message? Tell them you're here?" When Marian nodded, Pauline left the room.

"What's the something else?" Ted said.

"My skin."

Ted waited patiently.

"It's, well, something's happening to my skin. I can't swim in the pool anymore. If the kids see it they'll think I have some terrible disease. They'd be scared to go in the water."

"It's that bad?"

"It's that bad. If I saw it on someone else, I wouldn't want to go in the same water with them."

"Where? Your arms? Your legs?"

"All over. Well, not all over. Both legs. From my waist down to my ankles. It's like a rash, a really bad rash. The last few days it's been so bad I can't, you know, I can't wear anything because it snags."

"Snags on your rash?"

"Yes. It's like I have tiny splinters sticking out of me."

"Would you like to go home and I'll come over when Evelyn and

Robert come home and examine you there?."

"It's OK here. You can examine me here, Ted. I'm not embarrassed or scared of you. You know my body better than I do. And I don't want to scare Mom and Dad if it's not important. That's why I came now. It's happened so fast. Last week I was fine. Now, I...I hurt all over."

Pauline returned and said she'd left a message for Marian's parents.

"Marian's got a severe rash," Ted said. "Go ahead, Mare. Undress. But if they're so hard to put on, why wear jeans?"

"To hide the rash. Ted, I'm sorry. I didn't even call to ask if I could talk to you. And your dinner..."

"Hush," Pauline said. "You take off those jeans. You need some help, someone to lean on?"

"No, thanks, Pauline. I can manage. It just...takes...time...ouch... because they...ouch...catch."

Marian, with shoes and jeans removed, and wearing panties and a pale blue t-shirt, took a few steps to the two lamps Ted had positioned near a window.

Ted kneeled and examined her legs in the light, and then he had her turn around, her back to him.

The rash was a collection of minute, sharp-tipped bumps. Not blisters, not boils.

"Sit in the chair, Mare and extend your legs. Pauline, would you bring me that magnifying glass from my desk, please."

With the glass, Ted examined her feet, calves, and thighs. Her bare toes, he noticed, had still not lost their webbing. In fact, he realized that the webbing was actually more denser, slightly puffy, yielding to pressure of a fingertip, and extending now more than halfway up between each toe.

"Yeah," Marian said. "I forgot that. They've come back."

Was he imagining it or were her feet turned out more than they had been previously? X-rays and comparisons were, he knew, inevitable.

"Have you eaten anything new, anything different?" he asked.

"No. I'm still a strict vegetarian. In fact, I'm almost a vegan. Well, I do eat tuna fish. Almost every meal."

"Different kind of clothing? Wool or cotton or...?"

"Same ol', same ol'."

"OK. Let's say, for the moment, it's an allergic reaction. I'll set up an appointment for you with Irma Berlin. A dermatologist. Trained in Europe, lectures at Stanford and U.C. What's best for you, Mare? Saturday morning probably, right?"

"I can go anytime."

"Oh, right. You're driving now. OK, I'll call Dr. Berlin tomorrow morning. But I want to check your heart and lungs once more. Would you please take off your t-shirt."

"I'm not wearing a bra, Ted. I'm sorry."

"Mare," Pauline laughed. "Would you do what your doctor tells you to do."

Ted went through the process, with Marian anticipating his directions for breathing and coughing before he spoke them. After four or five minutes Ted, said, relief audible in his voice, "No fluid. Victory. Now, about that pain in your legs. There's an orthopedic surgeon at the hospital. Dr. Gottschalk. I know he'll see you tomorrow if I set it up. Probably before Dr. Berlin, if possible. OK? You want some dinner?"

"No, thanks. Mom and Dad'll be home soon. I better tell them."

"Yes, I believe you should rather than me."

"Rather than I," Pauline said.

"We have too many wanna-be grammarians in our families," Ted said, winking at Marian.

Marian paused at the door and then returned to hug both of the Longacres. "Ted, I've never thanked you for everything you've done for me. Since the day I was born. Can I write to you if I go away, you know, to college?"

"Me, too?" Pauline said. "Or am I to be the 'other woman' in this family?"

When Marian, near tears, hugged her, Pauline said, "Oh, my dear near-daughter. You know, Marian, that if I could, I'd adopt you. It would-n't be too hard for you. Your mom and dad will be living right next door."

After Marian closed the door, Ted returned the lamps to their original sites. "I'm worried, Pauline," he said. " I'm *very* worried."

≈≈

Marian decided she would tell her parents at dinner.

She didn't.

Instead, she'd tell them when she returned from Kathy's house where she said she was going to study.

Robert asked what Mr. Study looked like and was he rich enough so her weary, devoted, hard-working, and impoverished father could retire earlier than planned.

Marian and Kathy, actually did study. Or tried to.

Kathy needed background noise whenever she and Marian weren't talking, and tonight she relied on television rather than her CDs.

Channel 4. Then Channel 5. Then Channel...Wait. Back to Channel 5.

Marian, considering the formula for the square of the hypotenuse of a right triangle, heard behind her back the words *special bulletin* and then the word *whale.*

"Several people," the reporter said, facing the camera, "on shore and in launches, are trying to provoke the whale into a return to the bay but..."

Marian left her trigonometry book and stood in front of the television set.

"Volunteers from the Sea Mammal Rescue Center have arrived in two boats. They are going to try to work their magic to save this whale."

On the screen was a mass of row boats, canoes, and motor launches, as well as people wading in and swimming around the mammoth whale floundering at this moment in the waters of the Sacramento River.

"The whale, a Humpback, has been dubbed Humphrey," the reporter said. "Now almost a mile up the river, a mile out of the deep waters of the Bay, Humphrey, if he's not turned around and if he's not persuaded to swim back down the river, could die here in this unlikely cemetery. Experts from the Rescue Center tell us that in such shallow water a whale's respiratory and circulatory systems could simply shut down...simply collapse. Humphrey could die right here in the Sacramento River."

"Let's go," Marian said, grabbing her jacket.

"Go where?"

"We're driving to the river. We're going to help that whale. Some idiot named her Humphrey."

"Wait, I really should tell Mom. No, damn it. If you go, I go. But how do you know it's a her?"

"You saw her. She's a her."

Two hours later, unable to move in the stalled traffic, Marian swung her car into a side street, parked and ran, Kathy following, thinking she better work harder on those leg-lifts at the gym tomorrow.

Kathy Lumley was to recall the event years later in an interview on National Public Radio. "There were more media trucks and lights and cameras and media geeks rushing around than if the President and Abraham Lincoln had been wading in with the other volunteers."

Police had erected rope barriers and were patrolling with dogs to keep the media and the crowds away from the workers struggling in the water with the whale.

Marian pulled off her shoes and jeans and shirt, and wearing only panties, leaped into the water. She moved faster than the two cops and even their dogs, speeding past the three official boats of the Rescue Center.

At least twenty people were working with the whale, stroking, rubbing, pushing, pulling. Several ropes had been wrapped about the huge beast in an apparent effort to rig some sort of net that might be pulled by one or more of the larger boats. But all that had been accomplished was to ensnare the whale in a mesh that was probably choking her.

Marian grabbed a long knife from a man leaning into the mass of gray-black flesh and began slashing the ropes. "You're choking her," Marian shouted. "You're killing her."

Then, gliding to the cavernous mouth that was opening, closing, whispering groans, Marian moved her hands and arms through the curtains of creamy white baleen until she formed a space where she could sound her chirps and clicks that shaped themselves into melodies that came naturally now.

The song, made of sounds and colors around them, promised the whale that this strange creature, this sister, this hair-topped, four-limbed land creature struggling to sing in an alien language, could be trusted.

In California, North Dakota, Ohio, and New York, in every state in the union and in every province in Canada and South America and Europe and Asia, people watching television saw the whale suck in such a large portion of the young woman's body that every viewer was sure this female Jonah was doomed.

But then...

The whale opened her mouth and the blond-haired nearly-naked young woman swam free of the mouth. Pushed, prodded, tickled, and caressed by the young woman, the huge gray-black whale turned very slowly and faced south.

The mountainous whale, apparently not just obediently but happily, followed Marian down the river, its great tail rising every few moments to slap the water either in joy or impatience and blow huge sprays of spume into the air.

The other volunteers in the water stayed clear of the whale and Marian, leaving them free to do what they pleased in whatever amount of space they needed to do it.

As the whale approached the bay and the river water deepened, none of the volunteers in the boats could keep pace with the whale or the young woman.

No horns blared, no voices called.

One after another, the volunteers fell behind. The young woman then stretched out on the back of the whale as it moved south through the water toward the waiting San Francisco Bay.

Thanks to the cameras on the banks of the river and the Bay, the world saw Marian lead that great gray-black behemoth into the bay and under the spans of the Golden Gate Bridge into the ocean where, several days before, this whale's many families had passed and had somehow lost this young aquatic adventurer.

Viewers watched as, once in the open waters of the ocean, Marian, atop the huge head, slid off into the water, lingered for a moment and then started swimming toward shore.

The whale raised her tail, dove down and disappeared. Minutes later, she reappeared to breach. To offer a grateful spume and a trumpeting thunderous whoosh of joy!

Or was it gratitude?

Marian turned to wave as the whale swam south.

She waited off shore, treading water, until the whale disappeared from sight.

Radio, television, newspapers all over the world covered the event in the Sacramento River in California. Wars, plagues, political corruption played fourth or fifth fiddle to the story of the young woman who entered the mouth of a whale and then led that whale to a new life.

Marian refused interviews with officials at every oceanographic society in the United States and fourteen other nations. She refused to talk to an official from the Department of Defense, whose instructions were: "Get that girl! Offer her family a fortune and a home in Florida! Play on her patriotism! This young woman offers her country a new arsenal of weapons!"

A famous Hollywood producer phoned to say, "Miss Conroy, you can name your price. You name them, we'll get the stars for this movie."

"No, thanks."

The most famous literary agent in New York said, "Your signature would mean mega-bucks, Mrs. Conroy. We could get you a billion dollars."

Marian's mother said, "No, thanks."

When the agent whispered over the phone to Robert Conroy, "We have to talk. I mean talk money," he said, "My daughter says 'no, thanks.'"

〰

At the end of that memorable night, after dropping Kathy off at home and wishing her luck with her probably angry mom and dad, Marian drove home to find her own parents switching from one TV channel to another.

It turned out Robert had heard the news on his office radio while sitting at his computer—an announcement of a developing story about a whale in the Sacramento River and a young woman. Before hearing another word Robert had shouted "Ev! Evelyn!"

As Marian walked through the front door, Robert, with a sigh of resignation, picked up the ringing phone and, insisting that he wouldn't talk to another agent or reporter or talk show host even if it were Jay Leno, *especially* if it were Jay Leno, then said to his son, "Oh, hi, Todd."

Robert handed the phone to Evelyn.

Evelyn said, "Yes, Todd, we've seen it. Tommy has too, he's called us twice. I don't know. We haven't talked to the Whale Woman yet but she just came in. Yes, that's what Peter Jennings, or maybe it was Dan Rather, one of them, called her. The whale-woman. I'll tell her. She'll probably call you later tonight. The phone's been ringing off the hook all evening and I have the feeling it's going to be like this until sometime next year."

The moment Evelyn hung up the phone it rang again. She lifted the receiver. "Thanks, Ted. Yes, we've been watching. Actually, that might be a rescue operation for the Conroys. For the older Conroys at least. See you in a minute."

Evelyn annound, "Ted just got home from the hospital. He heard it on the car radio. He suggests we join them for coffee and whatever's in the freezer. He thinks we better talk about all this. Marian, it's up to you. You and I have to talk very soon if not now. You want to go over?"

"I guess I should," Marian said.

"Do you have anything to say to us first?"

"No. Why?"

"Well, I can't be quite as blasé about all this as you seem to be," Evelyn said.

"We're worried," Robert said.

"What's to worry about?"

Evelyn shook her head. "I'm finally beginning to believe you're honestly as innocent as you act, Marian. You're not pretending. You have any idea what's happening?"

Marian sat there blinking her eyes like an innocent child suspected of having stolen a cookie. Then she lowered her chin and, her voice trembling, said, "I'm scared, Mom."

Her mother, in tears, held her and said, "Me too, baby."

Robert began to feel just the first symptoms of fear about...about what?.

"Should we have our talk before or after we go to the Longacres?"

"We ought to have it there," Marian said. "With Ted and Pauline."

〰

Robert started it off with an analysis of motive. Not Marian's, the media's.

The media would use his daughter to peddle products. He and Evelyn would not permit that.

Pauline Longacre had no interest in analyzing; she could only say that she'd been in a state of hypnosis since she'd seen the first image of Marian Conroy's face and naked body sliding into the humpback's mouth. "My God," she said, "you were naked."

"I was wearing my panties."

"You were not. You were naked."

"Maybe they came off when I..."

"When you played Miss Jonah for that whale?" Robert asked.

"Dad, you aren't funny."

Robert said, "I'm sorry, Mare. It's just that I'm not quite adjusted to this new role of cynic and protector and admirer all rolled into one. Oh, add father to that."

He looked at Evelyn, who was leaning against the back of an armchair. Gazing up at the ceiling, she was hoping, praying for a sign. A sign that she had been waiting for ever since the birth of this child. Ever since that moment the nurse had lifted the little bundle of wrinkled flesh and said,cheerfully, "A girl, Mrs. Conroy! You have a daughter!"

"Marian, what is this stuff about you talking to that whale, persuading it..." Robert began.

"Her."

"Sorry. Persuading her to follow you? Did someone pay you to do all this? Was this whole thing a Hollywood production thought up by some

TV wiseass?"

"No one paid her," Evelyn said. Her voice was calm and quiet. "She did what we and millions of others saw her do. Marian couldn't *not* have done what she did."

All of them turned to Evelyn in various stages of apprehension or shock or both.

"We have a lot to talk about," Evelyn said.

Marian, who was drinking ice water, said, "Yes, I want to talk. But I've got to get something first. Be right back."

In the kitchen she sprinkled salt into her ice water and returned to the living room, drinking her heavily-salted water.

"Ev?"

Robert was challenging his wife to say something that would clarify matters. But before Evelyn could speak, Marian said, "Sorry, Mom, but before you say what I know you want to say, I have to speak."

Then came the first and last explosion her father ever permitted himself. "How the hell do you know what your mother wants to say? Are you suddenly possessed of mystic powers?"

"In a way," Marian said. "I guess, in a way, I am."

Evelyn stared into her hands folded in her lap.

Marian cleared her throat. "I came over here to Ted and Pauline's house this afternoon. Before you guys got home. I told Ted I'd tell you but then I just didn't. Or couldn't. I guess I had the feeling, no, it was hope. I guess I hoped it all might go away like it has before. But this time it didn't go away."

"What," Robert asked, "do you mean by *it*?"

"Patience," Ted Longacre murmured, "patience, Robert."

"Things are happening to my body, Dad. My mind, too. But right now mostly my body."

A tiny whimper escaped Evelyn Conroy.

"Ted made appointments for me with a dermatologist and with an orthopedist. I see them tomorrow. But I know what they're going to see. I even know what they're going to say."

Robert's eyes went from his daughter to his wife, who had a tissue to her eyes. He turned to Ted, who was peering down into his coffee, and to Pauline, who was watching Marian with such sympathy he thought for a moment she knew what was coming.

Marian pulled herself up from the cushion on which she had been sitting and walked to the sofa and stood before her mother and father.

"Dad, my legs are growing together."

He started to protest, even, perhaps, to silence, her, but his daughter's absolute certainty stopped him.

"My insides are changing, Dad. From human to...well, to fish. My body, from my ankles to my waist, is covered with what the dermatologist will call...what was it, Ted?"

"Contusions, but..."

"They're scratchy and itchy and look sort of like scales. Like fish scales."

Evelyn slowly stood up and walked to the telephone. Robert, knowing whom his wife was calling, held out his arms to Marian. She dropped down on the sofa next to him, laying her head on his shoulder. His hands touched her hair and he murmured, "My God...oh my God..."

Evelyn's voice hovered in the air like notes plucked from a cello string. "Mother?...yes, it's me...she's all right. It's hard, of course it's hard...yes, the phone's been ringing every second...we're at the Longacres...all right...we'll take her out of school for a week...yes, all right...no, Mother, let us finish talking here and then, tomorrow morning she'll call you...I know, I know...all my life, Talbot, all my life...thank you...oh Mother, you've been more patient with me than I've ever been with you, than I ever was with my brother, oh God, my brother Talbot...good night, Mother...I love you."

〰
〰

After breakfast the next day, Robert opened the door to Kathy Lumley and said yes, Marian was in her room and yes, of course Kathy could go on up.

Marian heard the doorbell and knew who was there. She was lying on her just-made bed, against a wall of pillows.

Kathy walked to the window and stood there, gazing down at the cliff, at the sea, wanting to talk but finding herself unable to.

Marian helped her. "You didn't know you had a monster for a

friend."

"Don't say that!" Kathy shouted, "You're..."

And then she was on the bed, holding Marian in her arms.

"Go ahead," Marian said. "I wish I could cry but I feel so relieved that I'm really not sad. And Kath, honest, I'm not scared. In fact, I'm almost sort of happy."

Kathy used Marian's bed-sheet to wipe her eyes and blow her nose. "Gee," Marian said. "Thanks a lot."

Kathy started to laugh but gave way to more painful sobs.

"It's complicated, Kath, but...well...all my life Mom has been waiting for this to happen."

"Your mom knew?"

"She never said she knew...never to herself...but she knew."

Marian leaned forward and grabbed her ankles. She spread her fingers. "Look. It's grown back. On the fingers and the toes. Thicker than ever."

Kathy touched the almost transparent skin stretching between thumb and index finger of Marian's right hand and then the skin between the large toe and the next toe of her right foot. "Syn...syn what?"

"Syndactyly. That's the medical term. The other term is..."

"Is what, Mare?"

"Mermaid," Marian whispered.

"My God, Mare. Mermaid? Are you scared, Mare?"

Marian shook her head. "I'm not scared at all. Honest. The farther I go, I mean the less human I get and the more mermaidey, the more I'll have to be away from this house, from my family, from you, well, it's sort of like growing up. Everyone knows they're getting older but they can't do anything about it."

"How long...when...?"

"I don't know," Marian said. "No one knows. I might be around exactly like I am for another fifty years or I might kick off tomorrow."

"Will you...oh God, Mare, you mean *die*?"

"Some day, yeah. But so will you."

"Will you have to stay in bed now? Your mother told my folks everyone wants to interview you, wants make movies about you, put you on TV..."

Marian pretended to be taken with the idea. "Hello, Oprah," she said, holding an imaginary microphone. "Yes, I swim a lot. My favorite food? Herring. Oh I just love herring. Do you know, Oprah, that Dutch herring are better than German?...Oh hello. Chef Emeril. Green algae? Oh my, Chef, green algae is great with fresh octopus gizzard."

"Stop it, Mare," Kathy said. Then, turned serious, "Will you have to stay in bed? Use a wheelchair? I'll stay with you, Mare. I'll push you wherever you want to go."

"I'll be able to walk for a while. Don't know how long. But there are some things I know I'm going to do first."

Kathy waited, eyes wide.

"First, you have to promise me something, Kath."

"I'll promise anything, Mare."

"Mom and Dad are letting me visit Grandma. I'm taking off from school for a week. Can I call you from Maine whenever I feel like talking to you?"

〰〰

Marian called the Marine Mammal Rescue Center and asked to speak to the director.

A woman answered somewhat impatiently, "Lu Herold."

"Hello, I want to volunteer for the Rescue Center."

"Oh, sorry. The operator's new; she should have connected you with..."

"You're the director, I want to talk to you. Someone else will put me off because I'm not eighteen yet. I know you have to be eighteen to..."

"Right. Let me transfer..."

"My name's Marian Conroy. I was on television news report. With the whale."

"I'm sure the oper...Marian Con...is this really Marian Conroy?"

"Yes."

"The one on the program with the Humpback...you're that Marian Conroy?"

"Yes, that's me. I'm going away for a week and then I'll be back but I want to be sure it's all set up for me to work at the Rescue Center when

I get back because things are happening so fast…"

"Things? What sorts of things? In a week? Could you come down today? We can talk. I want to call the newspapers and…"

"No. That's why I'm calling. No newspapers, no cameras."

"Miss Conroy, we survive on contributions. Your coming here could help us a great deal by…."

"No. In that case I'll do it alone. Out in the ocean. I'll just help them by myself."

"Them?"

"All of them. I thought you'd want to help them, too."

"Wait. Don't hang up. Tell me. How old are you exactly, Miss Conroy? May I call you Marian?"

"Sure. I'll be eighteen in five months."

"Where do you live?"

"San Francisco."

"Do you know how to get here?"

"I'll find it."

"Would your folks sign a waiver absolving the Center from any responsibility if you get hurt? Or maybe we can set you up so you don't go near the animals. We do that with high school volunteers. They clean up and do office work, that sort of stuff."

"No office work. No. I work with them, whoever's sick or hurt. I only work with them. And my folks will sign a waiver so you won't be sued if I get hurt."

"Will you call when you get back from your trip?"

"Yes. I promise."

"How about starting here two or three days after you return? But I'll need an address so I can send the papers to your parents. You can bring them when you come here. Marian, trust me. I won't tell a single reporter."

〰〰

"Kath, hi. It's me."

"Hey, Mare. What's happenin'? We haven't talked for ninety-four minutes."

"I'm doing it. I'm going to Maine tomorrow."

"Great! Well, I hope it turns out perfect. Wish I was going with you."

"Me, too. But I have to do this alone. Just about had all my own hair pulled out by the time I convinced them I could travel by myself. But I worked on Todd and Tommy and they worked on Dad and Dad worked on Mom. She said absolutely not but then finally, after maybe a hundred years, she said OK."

"Well, hey, it's not like you're a world-traveler, Mare. That's what moms are for, right? To worry. This is the first time you've ever been on a plane alone. You worry me, too, Mare. I hope the pilot's a hunk, though. OK? I bet your dad said *no problema*."

"No. At first he agreed with Mom. I wasn't in condition to handle the problems alone. What if something happened with my legs or my lungs. He kept trying to convince me to at least let Todd and Tommy go with me. No way, Jose. Mom was harder to convince. That's when I kept pullin' out my hair and my toenails and my eyelashes."

"So it's a done deal. So I'm comin' over for dinner tonight, right? That still on?"

"Right, yeah, it's still on. And you're sleepin' over?"

"I'm countin' on it. But I just have to tell you. I'm bringing you a going-away-come-back-soon gift."

"Aw. What is it?"

"Can't tell you except you can bet it's not in a can and well, actually it is fishy. OK, I'll tell you. It's a book."

"A book? You, Kathy Lumley, *you* are giving *me* a book? Is it a book about tofu? *How To Cook and Eat Tofu and Keep it Down* by Kathy Lumley."

"It's a book about fish, smart-ass. Whales are considered fish, right?"

"No, but Kath, I bet I know what the book is."

"Bet you don't."

"I bet it's a book called *Sightings* and it has photographs of whales and one of the photographs is a newborn with its...what's it called?...its..."

"Its umbilical cord."

"Umbilical cord. I heard the author interviewed on the radio last night about midnight and I planned to buy the book because some of the things she said and the sound of her voice got to me."

"Mare, you are weird. But you are cool weird. It's the one, that's the book. I guess I won't have to worry about you going on a plane to Maine."

"I love you, Kathy Lumley. See you in seven hours and forty-four minutes and twelve seconds."

"Nine seconds. Like they say, or said, see you around, square."

"Oh, yeah. Later, alligator."

9

The blue commuter plane out of New York had been skirting the coast for an hour. The pilot's voice lifted free of the intercom static as the plane turned inland and began its descent. "It's 1600 hours in Maine. That's four o'clock in the afternoon to land-lubbers. We're five minutes ahead of schedule. Be prepared. It's cold on the ground. In the low 40s. How about mid-30s? High 20s? Please fasten your seat belts and remain seated until the plane lands, taxis to a complete stop, and I've turned off the engine. Thank you for flying Downcoast Airlines."

Marian, at one of the six window seats, put down her book and tensed her body in preparation for the impact, but all she felt was a slight bump. She tried to slide her book into her backpack but her fingers defied her. They were so numb she couldn't grip the zipper tab.

For a few minutes in New York, when she was trying to find her way through the traffic of LaGuardia airport, her fingers and toes had gone numb. A flight attendant, having observed her stumbling, had taken her by the arm and, even carried one of her bags as she walked Marian to the distant gate used by the commuter lines.

Imprisoned in her seat now, her fingers numb once again, she gave up struggling with her backpack. She would just have carry the book under her arm. Unless she could work her tricks again.

The pilot had told everyone to bring their seats upright, but now, her seat tilted back, Marian raised her arms above her head.

The woman next to her, in the aisle seat, leaned away to avoid being struck. "You better buckle your belt," the woman said. "The plane's still moving."

"Sorry I bumped you," Marian said. "My arms and my legs fell asleep."

Her arms hadn't fallen asleep. Nor had her legs. But there was a change.

The stretching had stimulated the circulation enough so her fingers could now grip the zipper tab. Once the pocket on her backpack was open and the book safely stowed, Marian put her seat forward and fastened her seat belt.

As the plane rolled to a stop, Marian concentrated on the faces of the people standing in front of the small terminal building. Audrey Bishop stood to the side of the crowd, alone, tall and erect, the cone of her gray hair balanced on top of her head.

≈

"The tallest and coldest mountain in Maine," had been Evelyn's description of Audrey Bishop. She hadn't realized the eight-year-old Marian had overheard the comment.

Eighty-four hours ago, when Marian heard Evelyn crying like a long-lost orphan who found her home, she was reminded of her mother's former scorn for her aged 3,000-mile-away mother, Marian's grandmother.

I love you, Mother.

Those were the words Evelyn had spoken aloud hours ago in the presence of her husband and her daughter.

I love you, Mother.

When Todd and Tommy arrived to wish her *bon voyage*, Marian had confided to them that their mother had said "I love you," to Grandma Audrey.

"She honest-to-God said, 'I love you, Mother.' And she cried. She cried real honest-to-God tears."

Todd: "Mom?"

Tommy: "Our cool I'm-a-detached-mathematician mom?"

"And something else. She apologized to Grandma for...she said, 'Mother, I apologize for all those years of torment.' "

"Our Mom apologized?" Todd said. "You sure it wasn't Dad with a head cold talking to Grandma?"

Tommy, wide-mouthed in disbelief, said, "Mom apologized? I'm goin' outside and check the sky because, man, there has to be a new star up there and maybe two moons. I wanna be the first to see the show."

～

Now, from the far side of the parking lot, Marian's beloved grandma—windbreaker jacket tight over her sweater, thin collar up around her throat—was studying the face of every passenger coming down the small plane's fold-down metal steps.

Rising from her seat, Marian felt a shock of pain from her waist to her ankles. The pain vanished as fast as it had appeared and she sighed, relieved, when she reached the exit-door of the plane. After stumbling on the first step, she gripped the rails and carefully placed her feet on the next steps. On the asphalt, Marian raced into those waiting grandmotherly arms that lifted her off the ground as if she were weightless.

They shared kisses and greetings for several minutes and then Grandma Audrey, carrying the smaller of Marian's two bags, led her granddaughter to a shiny old Mercedes crouched like a black panther in the parking lot. The driver, who had been waiting at the open trunk, hurried forward to relieve both Audrey Bishop and her granddaughter of the luggage.

"Eric," Audrey Bishop said, " this beautiful young woman is my granddaughter, Marian. You've heard more than you will ever remember about this child. Marian, this is Eric. My right hand, my left hand, my arms and legs. He's been with us since the day your grandfather bought this car...what was it, Eric?...twenty-two years ago?"

"Two months short of twenty-three years, ma'am."

"Impressed, Marian? He isn't an employee, he's family."

"Thank you, ma'am."

"Inside now, child. You aren't used to this weather. This is a typical autumn day, wet and cold."

"I'd rather have it cold than hot, Grandma."

"I forgot. Of course. Eric, hasn't the child grown since you last saw her?"

"Yes, ma'am. Remember, she wasn't two years old at the time."

"I was here before?" Marian said, thinking she might have forgotten.

"Fifteen years ago, my dear. I'd be very surprised if you remembered."

Once inside the car Audrey Bishop finally relaxed. Noticing Marian's problems with the seat belt she casually intervened. "Now," she said, "your turn to relax. We have a twenty-minute ride or perhaps longer if there are more than three cars on the road. You have a choice, my dear. Silence for comfort, conversation for information."

"I don't want silence, Grandma. I want to talk and talk and talk. I have a million questions."

"You are your mother's daughter. Be patient. By the end of our seven days together we'll have talked enough to publish our own encyclopedia. Just let me know when you need relief. First—the flight. You had no trouble? Of course not. I told your parents you were wiser than your brothers, my beloved grandsons."

"I won't tell them. The flight was fine. I read the whole way."

"And what were you reading, pray tell?"

Marian held up the paperback. "*Sightings*."

Grandma Audrey widened her eyes and nodded, impressed. "By Brenda Peterson and Linda Hogan. I know the book. In fact, too well. I think Talbot would have added that book to his library. You must know it even better than I, given your intimacy with the animals. Does it meet your standards?"

"It's the only book I could read beyond the first page. It comes closer to what I know is the truth than any other book I've tried to read."

"Do I hear a criticism in your voice?"

"No, no. It's just that the word *sea* and the word *mammals* don't mean...those are words humans thought up...the ani...we..." and Marian paused. "I wish I could thank the authors."

"Try writing a fan letter."

It's time.

"I can't write any more, Grandma. I just stare at my computer and I can't find the words and..."

"You will," her grandma said, putting her arm around her. "Relax till we get home. If you need a nap, your mother's bed is waiting. The bed your mother slept in when she was your age."

"I want to talk. I want to look at you and talk, Grandma."

"Talk it shall be. And we needn't restrain ourselves just because Eric is here. He and Talbot were close friends. He's family."

Eric raised his gloved right hand in a mix of wave and salute. "I won't listen, Marian. And even were I to overhear your conversation I doubt I would learn anything I don't already know." And, with that, he put on earphones, turned up the volume of whatever he was hearing, and increased the Mercedes' speed by perhaps two miles an hour.

"Eric listens to BBC and NPR," Audrey Bishop explained. She shifted her body to have a better view of her granddaughter.

As the Mercedes hummed along the narrow road, Grandma Audrey slipped off her black leather gloves and dropped them into her lap, where they lay like a pair of sleeping birds. She then took Marian's hands into her own.

Marian talked about the family while the tip of her grandmother's right forefinger traced and retraced the folds at the base of Marian's palms.

"Is this the new tissue, Marian?"

"Yes. It's puffy and it sort of burns. Not always. Like four or five times a day."

"It's softer than the scartissue." Then she turned both of her own hands to offer the palms to Marian's fingertips.

"I don't feel them, Grandma."

"It's been sixty years since my second surgery. Occasionally I think I feel them returning."

"What's it feel like? When you think they're growing again, I mean."

"I actually feel a scrambling activity beneath the skin. Like nervous little bugs trying to get out. But they've never returned."

"How old were you the second time, Grandma?"

"Seventeen, almost eighteen. Your age. But medical practice those years was...well, primitive would be a generous term."

"What would you do if they came back, Grandma?"

Marian, during the long pause, waited for a wise remark that might offer her guidance, but her grandmother was probably searching for words that wouldn't distress her granddaughter. Finally, Audrey Bishop said, "I'm seventy-six years old. If they were to return now I wouldn't have them removed." She took a deep breath. "I would appreciate them, thanks to you. You've altered my world. You've altered all of our worlds, Marian."

Grandma Audrey turned to gaze out the window. "I would take them with me at my death," she said, "as I brought them with me at my birth."

"Did your mom...your mother...have them, Grandma?"

"No. But her mother, *my* grandmother, did. I never knew my grandmother. In fact, I never knew *about* my grandmother until your Uncle Talbot...my grandmother had been long-buried when I was born."

"Todd and Tommy loved Uncle Talbot."

"He loved those boys. But he yearned to have you here, he dreamed about you visiting us. He waited and waited. He almost went to California just to be with you. Four or five times he, well, things were difficult. Talbot and Evelyn were always at odds about things."

"Mom told me about Uncle Talbot last night. About how she treated him."

"Yes, she told me about your conversation last night. You're to call her the minute we arrive home. They're all waiting."

"Did Uncle Talbot...was Uncle Talbot mad? Mom said she, well, she said she will never forgive herself. Last night she had all those old pictures on the bed, the pictures she brought back after his funeral."

"Talbot was the physical and spiritual image of your grandfather. A man of persistence, a man of precision. Fearless. If Talbot were alive now you'd find him a treasure trove of...well, if Talbot hadn't unearthed all the records, all the letters and all the diaries, I would probably never have learned what I now know about myself, about my grandmother, about..."

"About me."

"Indeed. About you. I bless him, as Evelyn does now."

"Tommy and Todd called him eccentric."

"That he was. But then your brothers have always considered me eccentric too. So has your mother, and until three nights ago not just eccentric. Your little escapade on television was the shot heard round our world. I was watching, and I called your mother. They were watching too. We were with you every moment you were with the whale, my darling. It changed their world, it changed my world. It verified the world

Talbot almost knew."

"It changed my world."

"*Especially* your world. And I'm relieved and, well, saddened. Desperately saddened. There is no evading the consequences to all our lives. Yours and ours."

"I wish everyone could feel like I do, Grandma. I'm not scared or sad. But I have to ask you about Uncle Talbot's house. Dad calls it *the warehouse*. He was there. The boys were there, too. They called it weird and spooky."

"A fair description. After Talbot returned from Vietnam and moved back into the house we both had been born in, he earned money lobstering. He owned three boats. He didn't have to work. He had a fair disability pension. Vietnam. After that experience with…"

"…the mermaid. Todd and Tommy told me about it."

"It changed his life. And mine. He became obsessed. That was his word. Evelyn's word was *demented*. She was furious. With both of us. But if it weren't for Talbot's obsession, I would be as ignorant as your mother has so unsuccessfully tried to be."

"I want to know everything, Grandma."

"What a wise old sage my darling grandchild has become in her youth."

Her laughter made Marian laugh too.

Eric turned his head and said, "That sound is more beautiful than the Bach I'm listening to." Then he returned to his role as chauffeur.

"You'll be with me for one week," Grandma Audrey said. "Actually, six days. I'll think of this time as your well-deserved rest and recuperation. R and R. That's the term your Uncle Talbot used. How rapidly these six days will pass."

Marian leaned back against the door and as she closed her eyes, she tried to untangle her emotions. "So, my great-great-grandmother had syndactyly," she said. "Do you look like her? Do I?"

"You will see very old and very faded photographs of her. And sketches and drawings. And an oil portrait over Talbot's desk which might be visible behind the stacks and beneath the dust blanket. My great-grandmother's great-grandmother concealed her webbed fingers and her webbed toes."

"Tommy and Todd, if they were here, would say, 'Way cool, man.'"

Audrey Bishop said, "Cool. I doubt my great-grandmother was ever *cool*. Of course that would be about the time of Nebuchadnezzar. The phenomenon now called *syndactyly* didn't have a name then. Thanks to Talbot we...I, your mother...we now know a great deal. You now know more than we will ever know. Does that knowledge help, Marian?"

"None of that matters to me, Grandma."

"If you were to have children..."

"I won't be having children, Grandma."

Audrey Bishop's response was part sigh, part grunt, as if she had been struck in the chest. She took some deep breaths. "When did you start realizing what is happening inside your body, Marian? Is realizing a fair word to use?"

"I guess that's an OK word."

"There must have been one moment, a singular experience."

"There was. That first night they called me to come down from the house to the water, to go out into the waves and join them. They sang to me."

"They."

"You can call them whatever you want to call them, but they talked and sang to me and I knew what they were asking me, what they were telling me. *Come home, come back, come back to us.* I heard that. Not in words—in songs."

"Oh, Lord! And you aren't at all frightened of what you now know?"

"Nope."

"You have no urge to hide, to beg Dr. Longacre to help you live on, to marry, to be a mother, to have a family? To see your children grow?"

Marian took her grandmother's hand. "It's never going to happen, Grandma. It wasn't meant to happen. You don't have to worry or feel sad for me. I even wish I could hurry it up. I'm serious, Grandma."

Audrey Bishop reached across Marian's lap to wipe the fogged window. "You must see this, child. We are in the middle of coastal Maine, on the western shore of Penobscot Bay. Your Uncle Talbot lived here the last twenty years of his life. His home isn't visible from the road but it's just behind that place there on the shore. Do you see the wharfs?"

She rolled down the window for a clearer view.

Marian sat up and, said, "Oh, I love the smell. What's all that stuff piled everywhere?"

"Coils of rope, bait bags, netting, floats, traps—everything lobstermen need to survive. When they were children Talbot and Evelyn virtually lived on these wharfs. *Lobster* was a term as common in their vocabulary as *mother* or *father*. For Talbot, lobster made a better breakfast than waffles or pancakes."

During the next few minutes they passed two more wharfs and groups of men moving from wharfs to anchored boats.

When the car finally came to a stop, Grandma Audrey drew Marian's hand to her lips and, after lightly kissing the web between thumb and forefinger, said, "We are home, Miss Marian."

And there, on the crest of a green mound of lawn was a house many times the size of Marian's in San Francisco.

"Clapboard," her grandma said.

"Clapboard?"

"That's what the white wooden siding is called. Federal. That's the name for the design of the house. That gabled roof, those double-hung windows. The windows still have their original shutters, but Talbot replaced the old with insulated glass to reduce heat loss. There was nothing Talbot couldn't do. Come. Why don't you nap while I prepare our dinner? "Eric, would you please take Marian's luggage to her room? And would you and your wife care to join us for dinner?"

"Thank you, Ma'am, but no. Tonight, you remember, we're going to Portland for Pirates of Penzance. "

"Oh yes. I forgot."

Marian, lifting one foot and then the other, managed the first few steps but then she stumbled. Grandma Audrey helped her up the circular stairway.

A nightgown of soft warm flannel slid over her head. Her arms were eased into the sleeves, and she thought of her mother holding her three-and four- and five-year-old body close. She wanted to curl up and float inside her mother's familiar scent.

Grandma Audrey said, "This is your mother's nightgown. She has most of her college clothes in the closets.

"Back," Marian whispered.

Her grandma drew the orange duvet up to Marian's chin.

Nearly asleep, Marian murmured, "My back, Grandma. My back really hurts. And now...oh...now my chest. I wish..."

10

"Hello. Pauline here."

"Pauline Longacre?"

"Yes. Who is this?"

"This is Audrey Bishop, Evelyn Conroy's mother. Marian's grand-mother."

"Mrs. Bishop, my God, yes, Marian's...something's wrong."

"Yes, Pauline. Is the doctor home? And please, it's Audrey. You both have been family for as long as I've known you."

"Yes. Pauline. We feel the same, Mrs...Audrey. Ted's at the hospital. Give me your number, please. I'll reach him on his cell phone immediately."

Audrey Bishop closed the door to Marian's room, Evelyn's old bedroom, and descended the stairs very slowly, suddenly struck with old age, with weakness, with instability. She managed to measure tea and boil water. With her pot of tea in her favorite tea-cozy, she settled herself near the kitchen phone, restraining the ache in her heart but not the tears in her eyes.

The phone rang as she was pouring her second cup.

"Dr. Longacre."

"Yes. Mrs. Bishop?"

"Audrey."

"Audrey, I just got the message. Marian's with you and you're concerned about something and it's serious. Tell me."

"I am very concerned. She arrived three hours ago. She was nearly asleep when we got home from the airport, and I had to help her up the stairs. She's sleeping now. As she was falling asleep she was hallucinating.

Her exact words were, '*my back, grandma, it really hurts and my chest.*'"

"Mrs. Bishop, Marian must come home as soon as possible. Tomorrow at the latest. Can you manage that? If not, I'll talk to Robert and Evelyn and one of us will leave tonight for Maine."

"Thank you, Ted. A friend of mine—I'm on the board of his corporation—has a private plane, a Lear jet I believe it's called. I have exploited his generosity before. Oh, forgive me for rambling. I will bring her home tomorrow. I'll make the arrangements. Now I better call Evelyn and Robert."

"Let me prepare them, Audrey."

"Please do. I want to be upstairs now with Marian. But I should know if she is taking any medication and if I should call my doctor."

"She is taking no medication. And, given what's happening to her, no physician who's not familiar with her history could possibly help her."

"Her history. Yes, her history. *Our* history."

"I agree the word *our* has to be stressed. But I assure you Marian's best chance for relief, her only chance, is here. At home. You do know, Audrey, that relief, all relief, is temporary?"

"I know that. From my conversation with Evelyn last evening. Tell me, Ted, tell me about Evelyn, tell me about my family."

"All of them, and Pauline and I are simply standing by, waiting to do whatever has to be done for Marian. We all know it is near the end."

Near the end.

"We're the only ones who are devastated, Audrey. Marian, when she's not in pain, is probably the happiest human being in the universe. Now, before we end this call, please stay with me a few more minutes. Tell me as much as you can. Start at the beginning, when you picked her up at the airport."

≈

"Kath?"

"Hey, Mare. Where are you? You still home? You didn't go to Maine?"

"I'm here, in Maine, with Grandma. But things are, well, strange, Kath'."

"It's nine o'clock here. So that makes it…what?…in Maine?"

"Midnight. I'm talking real quiet because Grandma's sleeping downstairs on the sofa. She was up here but then she went down. I woke up and found her asleep. I covered her with a blanket. I tried to call Eric but he's gone somewhere. I don't know what else to do."

"Eric who?"

"He's her chauffeur. Actually her friend too. But wait, I have to concentrate. You have to know something. Oh yeah, we're flying back tomorrow. She woke up for a minute and told me."

"We?"

"Grandma and me. It hasn't been easy, Kath."

"Hey, what time tomorrow?"

"I'm not sure. I know Grandma called Ted and then she called a friend who owns a plane. His pilot's flying us out to San Francisco tomorrow. Just Grandma and me. Nonstop. I'll know the exact time in the morning and I'll call you then but I was hoping you can maybe…"

"Stay over tomorrow night?"

"Yeah. Can you? Please, Kath'?"

"No problem, Mare. Mom and Dad know what's happening. They talked to your dad two or three times. They're cool about the whole thing, I mean my mom and dad are. So let me know what time. But Mare?"

"Hmm?"

"You having, you know, like, body things?"

"Body things, head things. I'm feeling pretty good right now. I might feel good for the next four or five days. I can't predict. But I have to do one thing before we leave. It'll be OK with Grandma, I think."

"What?"

"I have to go to my Uncle Talbot's house and I want to be there as long as I can. He was here tonight, he talked to me."

"Who?"

"My Uncle Talbot."

"He's dead, Mare."

"Uncle Talbot was here, Kath. He leaned over my bed. It was my mom's bed long ago. I could smell Mom in the nightgown and I could smell Uncle Talbot. He smelled like the sea. I better hang up, I hear

Grandma downstairs. I think she's coming up."

"Wait. Mare?"

"You love me. You were going to say you love me."

Kathy said sobbing, "So I don't have to tell you now?" She tried to laugh.

"You don't have to tell me. I know, Kath. I love you too."

"OK. I won't tell you. But there is something I do have to tell you."

She was crying harder but then, in control, she said, "When you go, when you leave us, Mare, a whole big chunk is going out of me, a whole great big great big chunk. Oh, Mare."

"Hey. Hey, Kath."

"OK, OK. Yeah? I'm an idiot."

〰〰

The minute Marian came skipping down the stairs her grandma offered her a glass of the cranberry juice she had made from her own berries.

After she had drunk it, Marian followed her grandmother out to the Mercedes.

"We're going to the Victorian by the Sea. For breakfast, of course. And doesn't my granddaughter look spry and beautiful this morning, Eric?"

"She does indeed, ma'am. As does, I must say, her doting grand-mother. Marian, the last time I saw you, your eyes were almost closed. They're wide open this morning, I'm happy to note."

"I feel great. Maybe I can study hard and be a cheerleader next year. Oh, I forgot. I'm graduating."

"Now will you please indulge your doting grandmother and wrap that scarf around your neck?"

As they passed the wharfs Marian rolled down the window just long enough to inhale the aromas and to wave at the men on the boats and then, laughing as her grandmother exaggerated the chattering of her teeth, she closed the window.

At the inn, Eric chose to wait in the car.

"Aren't you hungry, Eric? I'm starved," Marian said.

"I had my breakfast an hour before you fell out of bed, Marian. I'll stay in the car. The news is the best part of the BBC's morning program."

At the front door the owner hugged Audrey Bishop and stepped back.

"Ginny, meet my granddaughter, Marian. Marian, this is Ginny Lorenzo, a dear friend. Your Uncle Talbot came here for breakfast just about every day. I insist you taste Ginny's Maine wild blueberry pancakes."

"And just for you, Marian-from-California, my bread-of-the-day is my world-famous cinnamon sour cream coffee cake," Ginny said,

Audrey Bishop winked at her granddaughter. "What do you think, Marian? Does it appeal to you? You actually have no choice. I am insisting."

"Both of them," Ginny told Marian, "my blueberry pancakes and my coffee cake, were your uncle's favorites. Talbot would have breakfast here and then spend all day at the museum in Penobscot and then have lobster steamed in sea water with an ear of corn at the lobster pound on Lincolnsville Beach. He'd sit on their patio and watch the lobster boats and the ferries traveling back and forth to Islesboro until dark. Same routine every day, seven days a week. I loved your Uncle Talbot. I could depend on him."

Marian said. "OK. The blueberry pancakes and the coffee cake. But no coffee, please. Just water. Ice water."

When they were alone, Grandma Audrey said, "We don't have time or I'd have Ginny show you the house. 1881. The entire third floor used to be servants' quarters. There's a hidden servant's staircase that goes from the butler's pantry to the third floor."

"Next time," Marian said, laughing, and then, when she saw the pain in her grandmother's eyes, she said, serious now, "How long do we have before we have to be on the plane, Grandma?"

"We need to be at the airport in exactly three hours."

"Would Ginny be mad if we sort of rushed through breakfast? I wanted to go to the museum with you but now, well, I want to spend the whole time, all the time we can, at Uncle Talbot's house. I dreamed about Uncle Talbot last night. He talked to me. In my dream, I mean. Told me things that...did he ever sleep in Mom's room?"

"My dear child. He stayed in the house for two years. The two years after Evelyn went to college. Evelyn doesn't even know that. And he told you? Last night?"

"Yeah. And he told me about that widow's walk outside the bedroom. He said all those stories about widows walking out there and watching for their husbands' fishing boats coming back were, I forget the word."

"Myths?"

"Yeah, myths. He told me what to look for in his house."

"There is much to see. And no, Ginny won't be offended."

〰〰

Marian stood with her grandmother gazing down the sloping field to the wharfs on the edge of the bay. "I could just stand here all day and smell," Marian said.

"You mean breathe," Eric said.

Marian laughed. "I bet Uncle Talbot smelled."

"Both," Eric said.

Marian laughed again, as did her grandma. "Oh," Marian said, "but look at the view he had every day, every hour."

"He wouldn't live anywhere that didn't have the sight and sound and smell of the sea."

"That's why he hangs around, I guess," Marian said.

"Hangs around?" Eric repeated, arching his eyebrows at his employer.

"Meaning *his spirit hovers*, Eric. I won't be but a few minutes," Grandma Audrey said.

"I'll wait in the car, ma'am."

Audrey unlocked the door, and stepping inside, Marian at her heels, she sniffed and sneezed. "I must have the house cleaned again. Once a month isn't enough."

Scattered on the floor was what looked like a year's worth of mail, slipped through the slot in the heavy door but actually, the mail from less than a week. "Smells like old library paste," Marian said.

"Quite an apt description," her grandma said. "You go ahead and look around. I'll do a bit of cleaning up and fix a pot of tea. Or would you prefer...?"

"Ice water."

"Of course."

Marian had no interest in the house as architecture or as a place where she might or might not like to live or as a storage site for colonial furniture, which, her grandmother assured her, "Any museum would cut throats to possess."

"This stuff," Marian said, "all these books and all these papers and all these stacks of boxes. Wow!"

"Boxes containing books and papers and dust. Talbot Bishop greets you."

The books and the papers, even the dust, had been stored here, waiting for this very day when she, Marian, would arrive.

"Can you understand why your father calls this place a warehouse?" her grandmother called from the kitchen.

"Yeah, I sure can. What is all this stuff, Grandma?"

"Talbot-stuff. It was, it is, his life."

Grandma Audrey, standing near the front door, preparing to leave, was holding a saucer in one hand, a cup in the other. She sipped from the cup. "He haunts you, doesn't he, child?"

"All night last night."

"What would you like to do? Do you want to leave this mess and go to a real museum? The Marine Museum at Penobscot is half an hour from here. The curator is actually expecting us."

"How about you go to the museum and I stay here. I need to stay here and just, I don't know, just look around. Is that OK?"

Her grandma looked at her watch. "I'll be back in exactly sixty minutes. Then we can go home and pack and drive to the airport. Will you be ready in sixty minutes?"

"Make it fifty-nine."

"Hey, Grandma," Marian called as the Mercedes drove away. "I'll see you when I see you."

Her grandmother waved and Eric gave one brief beep on the horn.

Is this, Marian wondered, is this insistent person who takes my hand the moment my grandmother, the moment his mother departs, is this person tugging me away from the front door and into the dark hallway that leads like a dust-filled tunnel through the house to other rooms, is this person Uncle Talbot?

Yes, the whales told her, and *yes*, Marian heard the whales sing.

Is this Uncle Talbot who hovers here in this room, at this table where the CD player is?...Does he put the disk in the machine...to hear...the songs sung by her brothers and her sisters far out at sea? Is this Uncle Talbot?

Yes, Marian heard the whales sing.

Yes.

She read the front of the CD cover...*Choir of St. John the Divine, New York*...with which the whales sing as one magnificent chorus.

"Uncle Talbot?"

Marian's voice almost pulled her out of a doze to see Uncle Talbot going down the hall.

He played hide-and-seek now. "Uncle Talbot?"

The songs of the whales pulled Marian to the hallway that contained chairs and tables and desks, piled high with bundles of magazines and newspapers ready to topple at the sound of a whisper.

To the songs of the whales and the chorus, Marian drifted into dust-filled rooms where, on wall after wall, framed and unframed paintings and drawings and prints and photographs hung, waiting for her. Pictures of green lawns edged by ocean surf, of variations of faces and bodies of children mastering sails and winds and currents, of men bent double to fight the wind aboard their tilted boats consumed by black storms and green-black waves, of raging whales heaving up from the waves and...

...ah, Marian...here, just for you...

...a painting of...no, not a painting and not on the wall but on the floor, standing upright on the floor, in the center of the room...a body carved from stone.

A woman's body with a woman's face...a tail where legs might have been...a mermaid's tail.

"For you, Marian. All this...I've been waiting..."

Marian, inhaling the dust, felt ill, ready to collapse.

She was back now, ready to collapse, at the room where her grandmother left her and Uncle Talbot had taken command of her body and her mind.

Back in the chaos of dust and light and dark shadows was the song of the whales and the chorus of the Cathedral of St. John the Divine.

Back at the desk the whales and the chorus and Marian Conroy sang.

And as she sang Marian lowered her head into her arms and slept, or did she sleep...merely yearned for sleep? In her sleep or her dream she glanced down at the stack of notebooks she had been using as a pillow.

Were those notebooks here on this desk when she entered this house with her grandma or were they slipped into place now by Uncle Talbot? Covered with dust, they must have been here for months, perhaps for years.

Marian opened one notebook and the next and the next and she turned page after page.

Here were drawings and, pasted onto this or that page, pieces of articles from magazines or newspapers or scrawled messages in what must have been Uncle Talbot's writing that spoke with his voice, the handwriting that spoke like a voice, was like a voice, was Uncle Talbot's voice—*for you, Marian. I've been waiting. All this is for you...*

And on this fragment of paper: a drawing of a tiny baby...no, not a baby but a fish...no, not a fish but a baby...a baby fish...the drawing surrounded by concentric circles of words written years ago but spoken aloud this moment by dead Uncle Talbot.

1/10/97. 1435 hours brought up on a number 4 line a mermaid I took into my arms and held in my arms two minutes six seconds. I heard momma's voice and then grandma's voice telling me to return her to the sea.

I patted her face dry with my shirt and she squirmed in my hands and I kissed her face and slid her back down into the sea very gently and two minutes and three seconds after she dove beneath the surface and disappeared and she came back up and waved she was singing and she came up to the bow starboard and lifted her head out of the water and I put my face down near her and she kissed me on my lips and while she kissed me she somehow kept on singing and then she turned and dove head first and up came her tail and down she went again and she did not come back and I waited 2 hours 17 minutes and then I came home and told Mother and Mother nodded and said you better not tell Evelyn. But I did. I wrote Evelyn and told her and she called me and told me to never never never write her such things again.

On another page, in what must have been Uncle Talbot's handwriting: *from sea tales online by Kurt Cagle 1996 story called Ice about a sub in the arctic under the ice and the sailors hear a mermaid and the story reminded me of the same thing happening to me in the sea off the Vietnam coast. I forgot it until today reading this story. We were down forty fathoms and our sonar*

The rest of the writing was illegible, the ink was blurred.

In another notebook under a fading Polaroid photograph Marian recognized as one her father took of her (I was seven years old maybe?).

I told Todd and Tommy about the mermaid today and they laughed and just before they left to go back to California Todd gave me this photograph of Marian and I wrote to Marian about the mermaid and about the stories Mom has told me and stories and histories I have read and myths and folklore and other such things but Evelyn called me last night and said she had seen the letter addressed to Marian with my handwriting and she opened it and she said if I ever ever mention such things to Marian she will never speak to me again but I said she never spoke to me much all my life before that letter and I was sad about that. When I said those words on the phone she cried and hung up the phone and an hour and four minutes later she called again and asked me to forgive her and I should please try to understand that she is trying to protect her daughter and I said I do understand I do

On and on. Pages, notebooks, newspapers, magazines, pieces of pages, pieces of articles.

There were handwritten stories called, in Uncle Talbot's handwriting, *ghosts on the coast of maine by Carol Olvieri Schulte.* Story after story narrated by respectable citizens of local towns and villages, men and women who shared adventures with witches and ghosts and other strange phenomena.

There were underlined dates and times or circled notices of exhibits, all of them occurring at the Penobscot Marine Museum. *the exhibit including...in the old vestry 6/14 and 10/19...an exploration of real pyrates and why we have the image of them that we have...Storm at Sea, a quilt by Stonington Fishermen's Wives Co Op..."Working the Bay," an exhibit of life and industries, including fishing, ice harvesting, logging around Penobscot Bay in the 19th century..."Sails on Canvas," selected examples of original needlework designed and handworked by william whorf...*

Here was a mimeographed page from the catalogue from the Stephen Phillips Memorial Library about *"The Tale of the Mermaid" by Griffith, Lee Ellen, 1952—, an essay on the folklore and mythology of the mermaid accompanied by illustrations of objects from the exhibition...*

On a long piece of thick. still stiff parchment, *an ancient drawing of a whale (or is it a seal?) showing its skeleton which still contains perfect duplicates of human hands and human feet. Pieces and parts they no longer require to survive but refuse to give up.*

And here, in longhand, covering the page from edge to edge, a chart identifying nine languages and nine locations and in each of the nine languages the word that means *mermaid.*

Mermaid!

Ben-Vary from The Isle of Man; Ceasg, from Scotland; Dinny-Mara from the Isle of Man; Gwragedd Annwn, from Wales; Liban (called sanctified Mermaid whose form is seen in carvings in Christian churches); Lorelei, from Germany; Melusine (one of the most famous European Mermaids who had a double tail); Merro, from Ireland (whose appearance was dreaded because it heralded the coming of storms); Rusalki Vila (Russia and Slav countries; Tritons (Mediterranean Mermen).

Talbot circled the word *Mermen* and wrote above and beneath the words *Fulton Bishop note and sing this word with the choir and the whales.*

Mermen Talbot wrote. *And beside that written word another word also written: merman.*

"Diny-Mara," Marian said aloud. "From Isle of Man. Mar. Mar-ee-an. Marian."

Marian heard the door of the Mercedes slam. That was when, gazing at the dark wall through bleary eyes, she saw a large framed oil painting so dark, dust-covered. It might be a door, not a painting. But it was a painting. That is me, Marian told herself, that is me a hundred years ago, two hundred years ago, a thousand years, that is great-great-great Grandma.

"Marian? It's time, dear."

Marian felt her head being lifted. She worked to open her eyes and to keep them open. Had she been sleeping? Had she been dreaming? Had she...had she...had she...

"I'm so sorry, my dear. It's time."

"I'm ready, Grandma."

"Oh, sweet Lord in Heaven. You are so gray. Are you ill? Come, dear, Eric will carry you."

"I can walk, Grandma. I'm strong. I had a beautiful visit with Uncle Talbot. He held me and hugged me and told me stories about all sorts of things, Grandma."

11

At the San Francisco airport early Sunday afternoon, the cold December wind sweeping across the parking lot promised even colder weather ahead.

"I borrowed Ted's SUV," Robert said, "I knew we'd need plenty of room."

Evelyn and her mother sat in the third row seat, holding hands.

Robert drove to Cliffside Drive, asking about the trip, about everything Marian had experienced. Well, almost everything. When they arrived home Marian thought for a moment her father had driven to the wrong house. Christmas lights strung along the sidewalk wrapped themselves around spot-lighted banners ("Welcome Home, Marian" and "Greetings, Traveler!" and "Home is Where the Heart Is").

Marian followed her mother, Grandma Audrey, and her father into the house, trailed by Todd and Tommy. Out of the kitchen, wearing aprons, Ted and Pauline Longacre and Kathy appeared.

Throughout the almost two-hour meal (prepared, catered and served by the Longacres with help from Kathy) Marian recited carefully selected details of her three days in Maine. ("Uncle Talbot's warehouse," she told her father, "is really a warehouse.")

Not a word about the pains.

Not a word about stumbling.

Not a word about the nearly forgotten details of Grandma Audrey's house, the bedroom, her mom's flannel nightgown, Uncle Talbot's visit.

When Kathy said she'd better go home, Tommy and Todd flexed their muscles and offered to accompany and protect her for the seven long blocks.

The Longacres kissed Marian goodnight, and before leaving, went out with Grandma Audrey to the porch. They stayed there a good ten minutes before Grandma came in, her face haggard.

Marian, left alone with her mother and father, asked, "Anything new while I was exploring the world?"

"A Mrs. Herold called," Robert said. "Once yesterday, twice today. She's the Director of the Marine Mammal Rescue Center. She's waiting to hear from you."

"I'll call her tomorrow. I better go to bed now. I can hardly keep my eyes open. But Mom?"

"Yes, Mare?"

"Guess what?"

"I give up, Marianski."

"I slept in your bed."

Evelyn Conroy nodded. "Of course. And you found some old love letters under the mattress."

That wasn't what I discovered, Marian thought. But if she weren't so sleepy she might have invaded Todd and Tommy's territory to joke about the great mathematicians's romances.

"Hey," Robert said. "What about your aches? Different weather, different pains?"

"They came and went," Marian said.

"And now, this evening?"

"I ache a little bit. All over. And I'm beat."

"We'll walk you upstairs," Evelyn said. "And just like we used to do four days ago when you were a child, we'll read to you and we'll try hard not to embarrass you by trying to tuck you in. What will it be? The *Secret Garden*? The *Phantom Toll Booth*?"

"How about you both just sit there until I start snoring? I'd like that."

"I'd like that, too," Evelyn said, unable, unwilling, to keep her fingers from her daughter's hair, her cheeks, her chin.

"I'd rather hear Marian Conroy singing her version of "Bedbugs," Robert said.

"Sleep tight," Marian sang. "Don't let the bedbugs bite...I'm going, daddy."

"Don't let the bedbugs bite," her father sang, helping her along. "If they do."

"If they do…"

"I'll get a shoe…"

"I'll get a shoe and…beat them…"

"And beat them till they're black and blue. Good night sweet princess," Robert said. "May guardian angels sing thee…and all that."

Both parents stayed home the next day, telling Marian they had planned to. They knew she knew they were lying. All of them knew that their time together was now limited, that their time together could end in an hour, in a day, in a week. Whatever time there was would be spent together.

"Todd and Tommy will be home for a few days," Robert said.

"And Kathy," Evelyn said. "She'll be around. A whole big bunch."

After breakfast Marian dealt with the aftermath of travel: unpacking, laundry, contemplation, jetlag.

Mid-morning, she called the Marine Mammal Rescue Center.

"Mrs. Lu Herold, please."

"Lu Herold speaking."

"This is Marian Conroy."

"Marian, you're home early."

"Just a couple of days."

"Welcome back. You have a satisfying trip?"

"I did. Can I come down today? I have the papers my parents signed and I want to work."

"By all means. You're sure you still want anonymity?"

"That's my only absolute demand."

"You got it. We'll talk and I'll take you on a tour. You must know that if I introduce you by your name everyone will know you. They all talk about you without my having said a word about your plan to work with us. In fact, be prepared. They'll probably recognize you. What do we do about that?"

"I don't know. Let's see what happens. I don't want to sound like some famous Hollywood actress but you have to promise. No reporters, no photographers."

"Of course. I promise."

"I'll be there at noon."

"You know how to get here?"

"I'll find you. You're across the Bridge, just before I get to Sausalito."

"That's it. And Marian?"

"Yes?"

"I hope you're not disappointed in us. We're just a group of people concerned about the sea and everything that lives in the sea."

Marian heard a sound which, she realized, had come from her own mouth. It could have been interpreted as a sound of appreciation. But had it been her voice? It had been a low humming whistle inside her voice, a few sighs that, tongue up against the palate and snapping down, could have been mellow clicks.

〰〰

The road led into the hills, through the valley and then up a slight incline to the parking spaces and the buildings. And, barely visible from the parking area, the village of pens.

Marian could hear the calls of the seals and sea lions and felt, as she caught her balance after stumbling, that she might not be able to resist opening all the doors of all the pens and leading all the animals down the hill and into the Bay.

Leaving her car, Marian walked down a path that led, according to the sign, *to Office*. Lu Herold was waiting for her and opened the door before Marian could knock.

The office was small and cluttered and smelled of equal parts of pastries and sea-mammal effluvia.

"Can you tell me about yourself?" Lu asked, after pouring coffee for herself and water for Marian. "I'd be a liar if I didn't say I'm both an adoring fan and a potential cynic. Your fame precedes you and it's the sort of fame that gives me the creeps, to tell you the truth."

"I'll be upfront with you," Marion said. "I haven't even said these things this way to my mom and dad. They know about it but we just haven't talked about it. In detail, I mean. Well, what you're doing here is sort of...sort of helping me change without being scared while it's happening."

Lu Herold's feet had been up on her desk but now, very carefully, very slowly, one foot and then the other dropped to the floor. Her chair came upright. The expression on her face said, do I have a nut-case here?

"I'm not a nut case, Lu. You can talk to Dr. Ted Longacre in San Francisco. My neighbor. He's been taking care of me since I was born. And to my grandmother. She lives in Maine but she's at my home now. She came out to say goodbye. I'm her only grandaughter." Marian held out her hands. "My grandma had syndactyly when she was born. So did her grandmother. My mother didn't have it. I had surgery when I was born and had it again when I was five and then...well, it's climbing up my fingers and my toes faster every day."

Lu swallowed and her jaws worked and she tried very hard to appear trusting when obviously she was very suspicious.

"I might have a month or two to live here. Maybe a week or two. My body is changing. Fast. I can't stand meat, and I used to love it. I do eat fish, though. Do you?"

"Fish?" Lu said. "Certainly I eat fish, just as seals and porpoises and whales do. As fish do. I eat everything except humans. Can't stand the after-taste."

She paused. "Marian, I'm not sure..."

"Please wait before you toss me out or call the police. Please?"

Lu nodded. She considered this determined young woman who was not at all disordered or reluctant to talk of her impending death. But was it death she was really talking about? Or was it just a temporary delusional insanity to which she was surrendering?

Having observed the television coverage of Marian Conroy leading that Humpback down the Sacramento River to the bay and urging it on beneath the Golden Gate Bridge to journey south to find its family, Lu knew there was more here than a silly teenager seeking attention.

"OK," she said. "What's the story?"

≋

Leading Marian about the 30-acre site on the Marin County hillside Lu gave her a brief history of the Rescue Center, how and when it was conceived and how and why it has continued not just to survive but to thrive.

"We could house and care for fifty animals when I arrived three years ago. We didn't have the funds or the space or the workers for more than fifty. Now, thanks to a very strong support network, we have the funds for expansion. We have almost reached our limit in volunteer workers, we are constructing twenty new pens, we have three more veterinarians than we had three years ago, two of them specialists in diseases related to pollution. You've seen just about all of it, Marian. Do you have any questions?"

"No. I do have a confession. I won't do anything about it, I promise, but I do have to tell you. Every time we stopped and I saw these sick and wounded friends...the...ani...the friends...in the cages, I wanted to open the doors and push them down the hill to the Bay."

"I have that impulse so many times every day that I've gotten used to it. I don't feel guilty about it anymore. Those days when we load the release-boat with animals we've cured of disease or operated on so they can swim again, when we take them out to sea and release them, they almost sing when they dive off the boat and into the water. A water version of the Bible's prodigal son. And daughter."

"They do sing. When can I begin? Can I do something today?"

"I'll turn you over to Marty Gold. He's going to tube a very sick baby sea lion."

"Tube?"

"The baby's an orphan. Mother shot by fishermen. It hasn't eaten. Too weak to compete with the others in its tank for herring. It will die in a day or two if we don't get nourishment in it. So we'll be putting a tube down its throat into its stomach and tube-feed it. Marty's the best at getting the tube into the stomach and missing the lungs. If it gets in the lungs the baby could drown. You ready?"

"I'm ready."

"I have work I have to do. I'll check on you in an hour or two. But be prepared. I've been watching the people watching you. Everyone by now knows who you are. But they're understanding people. They'll leave you alone."

"Well, I can't do anything about attention except deal with it."

"How old did you say you were? Eighty?"

Marian, for the first time today, grinned.

Marty Gold showed Marian how to hold the pup while he inserted the tube down its throat.

Marian said, "Wait. You're choking him."

"Him?"

"Him. Let me..."

"You've never done this so..."

Turning away from Marty, Marian carried the pup to the edge of the tank. The pup, which had been squealing and fighting while Marty and another volunteer had been holding it, calmed down and, its huge dark eyes almost closing, settled back in Marian's arms at the sound of some strange deep-in-the-chest sounds Marty later told his friends he'd never heard before. "Not from any human."

Marty and other nearby volunteers heard Marian's, "*Quiet, baby,*" and saw the pup relax and permit Marian to insert the tip of the tube.

The languid pup, curled in her arms, lazily emptied the attached bottle.

The whole procedure, which normally would have taken half an hour, Marty reported to Lu, took less than ten minutes.

"After she was through...and I didn't even have to help, I didn't have to hold the pup or hold the bottle or fix the tube, anything...after she was through the pup lay in the sun and fell asleep. She called the pup a *him*. We named it Dinah. But I checked and she's a *him*, Lu."

Marian spent the rest of the afternoon cleaning pens and feeding herring to a big bull Elephant seal that had been blinded by a shotgun. For the three days of his confinement he had been attacking every volunteer that had tried to feed him. When Marian entered the pen (without the large *absolutely required* protection-board) and walked toward the bull, Marty and several volunteers ran to rescue her when the bull attacked, as it surely would.

They all saw Marian hold out a herring and they all saw the bull hump and lump forward, meekly extend his head and not so much growl as bark. While his mouth was open Marian slipped a herring onto his tongue.

As Marty and the others stood by in amazement, the bull barked ten more times, the mouth opened with each bark and Marian slid a single herring into the open long-toothed black jaws. When her pail was empty, Marian turned and left the pen.

Marty ran to close the gate, which Marian had left open.

At the end of the afternoon, as Marian walked by the office on the way to her car, Lu Herold called from her office window. "Wait, Marian. Wait a minute. We have to talk."

Marian waited by her car.

Lu put out her hand. "I'm not asking any questions or telling you anything," she said. "Maybe twenty volunteers came to me this afternoon, sort of in shock. They think you're a witch. There are animals here that have to be medicated before a vet can treat them and then there have to be three or four volunteers in with their boards to protect themselves and the vet. You went in with those animals alone and they rolled over and let you tickle their bellies. I'm not able to explain this. I just want to say thanks. No questions, no explanations. Every minute you can give us will be appreciated."

"But?"

"You knew there'd be a *but*. OK, yeah, there is a big but and it's probably mine."

Marian waited and then said, "You want me to sit and tape record my..."

Lu gasped and shook her head. "How did you know I was going to ask you that? How can you...Marian, you scare the hell out of me. You honest-to-God scare the hell out of me. Will you be here tomorrow?"

"I'll come every day if I can. Nothing else is, well, there's nothing else I want to do. Except, I better tell you, my back aches. And my legs. A lot. I might have to take a couple days off."

"Will you call me if you think I can help? I'll do whatever you want, whatever you need."

"Thanks. I know you will. But I better get home."

Lu and a dozen volunteers on the hillside watched Marian Conroy struggle to get into her car and drive away.

〰
〰

That night, at the dinner table, when Marian told her parents and her grandmother about her day at the Center, her grandma said, "How did you deal with the attention?"

"They left me alone. But, well, you better know something."

Robert and Evelyn and Grandma Audrey waited. Evelyn, who had been sitting across the table from her daughter, now came to sit beside her. "You're very pale," Evelyn said.

"Today," Marian said, choking on the word, "was sort of the best and the worst. I'm giving up, Mom. I can't fight it any more. I feel like I ought to say I'm feeling sick inside, because I am, but I, how do I say this, I also feel good about feeling sick. I think it's all going to happen soon."

"I'll call Ted."

"OK. And Mom?"

"Yes, love."

"I want you to love Grandma forever and I want you to remember how much you and Uncle Talbot loved each other."

Grandma Audrey had to excuse herself.

Robert said, "I'll call Todd and Tommy."

"I want Kathy to be with us, Dad. Can you call Kathy's mom and dad and maybe get their OK?"

Marian stood, almost fell, and then, as strong as ever, smiled and said she had to go upstairs. She wanted to lie down for a few minutes.

Robert called Kathy's parents and received permission for Kathy to stay with the Conroys for the next two, perhaps three, days. He called Todd and Tommy next and they promised to be home the next morning. Then he called Ted and Pauline.

~~~

Just before midnight, while Evelyn lay in bed weeping, and Robert tried unsuccessfully to console her, the phone rang.

"This is Lu Herold. The Sea Mammal Rescue Center."

"I know who you are. This is Marian's mother."

"Mrs. Conroy, I apologize for calling at this hour but there's an emergency. I need Marian's help."

Marian walked into her parents' room. "Is it Lu Herold? From the

Rescue Center?"

"She's right here," Evelyn said, offering Marian the phone with a shaking hand.

"Marian?"

"Yes. Hi, Lu."

"An emergency. I just received a call from an associate in Alaska. He works for Fish and Game. There's been a very serious earthquake there— 6.8 on the Richter scale. Mountain slides have closed off a huge lake that's been fed by the sea for a thousand years. Seals, porpoises, maybe even orcas, have been trapped. Hundreds. All kinds. Without access to salt water and food they can die. There's no way out. We're getting a rescue mission together. About twenty people. Two of our vets, three or four of my best volunteers, several strong workers. We're flying up tomorrow to see what can be done and if we can do it. If we need more help it's available up there. I want you to go with us. Can you?"

"I'll meet you at the Center. What time?"

"Contributions to the Center, past and current, will pay for this entire mission."

Lu Herold was addressing the twenty carefully selected passengers in the plane provided by Alaska Airlines.

"We land at Municipal Airport in Kodiak. Two charter operators, Island Air and Seahawk Air, have offered choppers to carry all of us plus our equipment from Municipal Airport to Lake Alutiiq. Latest information indicates the cliffs that collapsed during the quake not only closed off exit to the sea for all the animals trapped in the lake, but the mounds of earth, some as high as fifteen or twenty feet, will keep seawater from coming in. Meaning all the animals we don't get out are doomed."

Marian, sitting in the last row, at the window, bent forward as sharp pain pierced her stomach. She could almost taste the water in that lake, which, even as she sat in this plane, was turning into a solid inedible mass for those trapped *beasts*. No, not *beasts*. A brutal person was called a beast. Those animals in that lake were not *beasts*.

"All I ask," Lu continued, "is that you stay together. That you watch and support each other. It's going to be chaos down there and I'm getting reports there are continuing minor aftershocks. The ground is still very unstable. And in forty-eight to seventy-two hours there's a storm coming in. As much as we want to save these animals we have to be careful. We want to save ourselves, too. I have no idea what the dangers are. None of us will know until we land. But be prepared. It's cold, about ten degrees above zero, and it's windy and it's going to be colder and windier every hour we're working. Let's hope we can get an opening to the sea in twenty-four hours. Forty-eight at the most. No matter what, we can't stay longer than forty-eight hours. Again—keep an eye on each other. Also, very important—have your Mustang survival suits ready at all times."

Marian was in the last row, near the rest room. She had chosen that, and the others respected her desire to be left alone.

All except Lu, who now came down the aisle carrying two paper cups, one of steaming coffee, one of ice water with salt added. She sat in the empty seat next to Marian and offered her the water. "Exactly the mix you told me you liked."

"Thanks, Lu."

"Can we talk, Marian? For just a minute or two?"

"Sure."

"I received a report that there are one or two Humpback whales and one or two belugas in the lake. Several Steller sea lions and harbor seals. Ever see a beluga? I know you've seen a Humpback because Humphrey was a Humpback."

Marian shook her head. "Those are names people gave us...gave them. We don't...they don't have names for each other."

When she saw Lu bite her lip and blush she wanted to apologize, because she had heard herself use the word *we* when, at the same time she had said it she'd wanted to say *they*. She was, at this moment, neither one nor the other, neither a *we* nor a *they* . She knew too well that she was delicately balanced on a narrow line. "I'm sorry, Lu. I didn't mean to be a smartass. I keep taking it for granted that people will understand."

"Don't apologize. You're right. I just never thought of that. For someone supposed to be smart I can be awful dumb. Can I do anything to, well, help you with this, Marian? I can't think what it might be but if there is anything, anytime, will you tell me? Please?"

"Thanks, I don't think I need help but I don't even know what it could be, *help* I mean. But if I need to talk to you I'll tell you. There is something, though, something you better know."

Lu waited, forgetting about the cup of coffee in her hand.

"I'm beginning to be, well, not sick exactly, just...just hurting. In my legs and my gut."

"The minute we land in Kodiak you're going to the hospital."

"No. That won't change things. I'm staying with you, with everyone here. I haven't told you but my grandma, she's bringing the whole family up here. And Kathy Lumley, my best friend. And the Longacres, my doc...my doc...my doctor and his wife. They'll all stay out of our way, I promise. But they want to be here in case, well, in case I don't go back with them. To San Francisco. We might just say goodbye here."

She was having trouble now finding the sounds of words, sounds and meanings, fitting them together to...to what?

"Marian, please..."

"Don't feel sorry, Lu. I'm happier than I've been in a long time. I'm so glad I'm doing this...but there is this pain that probably means I'm getting ready for what I've been supposed to be getting ready for ever since I was born."

Marian held up her gloved hands and slowly removed the glove from her right hand. Between thumb and forefinger and between every finger the web of skin was thick and tough, reaching almost to the fingertip.

"My other hand and my feet are the same."

Lu closed her eyes and leaned back and did not try to stop or wipe away the tears. She left her seat, went into the rest room, disposed of her coffee, returned and leaned over Marian. "Thanks for trusting me with your, well, I can't call it your secret. That makes it sound as if we have an evil pact."

Marian laughed. "In a way it is evil," she said. "I could be called a traitor to people because look at me, I'm still people." She sighed. "For a while."

Lu squeezed her shoulder and went back down the aisle, answering questions from volunteers as she went.

Marian knew that the passengers had been selected for the various talents they had to offer, from the two veterinarians to the longtime veterans of other disasters, including the two men who looked like the Hulk, but were actually veterans of earthquake-rescue in Mexico, Turkey, South America, men who could manipulate every tool from a shovel to a crane to a giant earthmover.

"We'll be landing in fifteen minutes," Lu announced. "Just heard that local fishermen have donated four boats that will be taken to the lake by choppers offered by the Army Air Force. All four boats are thirty-eight-footers. They're rigged with radar, GPS, various electrical and mechanical systems, plus drift nets and winches. Now before you fasten your seat belts be sure your nametags are pinned on. Then fasten your seat belts and bring your seats upright. Just remember—this is something you'll be able to tell your grandchildren about. Oh, there'll probably be lots of media people. Ignore them. Judy, from our office, will deal with them, that's her job. Just be sure your face is clean and you don't have lettuce between your teeth when you smile. This is a high-class organization, folks."

No laughter, no applause, just silence.

Marian closed her eyes and composed a letter in her head that she knew would never be written, never be read.

*Dear everyone. Grandma, Mom, Dad, Tommy, Todd, Kathy, Pauline, Ted. I'm writing this letter now because we'll never talk to each other again...*and then she added *and dear Uncle Talbot we maybe won't even see each other again...*

As the plane started its descent, Marian's lungs almost burst. She didn't know how much more she could endure before crying out. But then by the time the wheels touched the runway the pain had diminished.

I think, she continued thinking she was writing, *I just got what divers call the bends, when they come up for air too fast...*

She would continue the mental letter later.

〰

There was no way to make the process pretty.

Time was just one of the enemies.

With a storm two or three days away and most of one day already taken with the movement of people and equipment from Municipal Airport in Kodiak to the lake, and darkness now approaching, a sense of possible failure grew rapidly to a promise of probable disaster.

While everyone else was setting up medical stations to care for the sick and injured, and receiving basic instructions on how best to use the boats and their owners, Marian was in the water.

Though everyone else was wrapped in weatherproof clothing that would keep them warm, Marian was almost too warm moving naked through the waters of Lake Alutiiq.

But move she did.

From seal to sea lion to whale to otter to seal to whale. All of their voices were plaintive, pleading to understand this new place that was denying them not just food but breath.

By now, three days after the quake, most of the fish and smaller marine animals had been hunted down and eaten by the larger. Were it not for a rapidly growing fatigue that was disabling every creature, even more of the smaller and slower ones would be eaten. All their natural nutrients, digestive and respiratory, were being more rapidly depleted every minute.

Lu and the veterinarians and the volunteers knew all this because such a consequence had been predicted by every expert at all the oceanographic organizations and government agencies in the United States. Marian knew all this because she just knew it—she felt it in her bones.

Lu waited for Marian's first report as she came out of the water two hours later. Wearing heavy boots and warm clothes, Lu had brought a parka to drape around Marian's shoulders but Marian shrugged it off, saying, "We might be able to trap or net a few of the smaller ones and carry them over the mounds of dirt to the sea and release them but most of them we couldn't manage even if we did capture them."

"Oh, my God," Lu said, not in response to Marian but in response to the sudden jerk and shake of the ground.

"Was that a quake?"

"That was a quake," Lu said. "I'm going to have to decide very soon if it's safe for our people to even stay here through today. We might just have to give up and go home. I can't take a chance." She touched Marian's naked arm. "I know you must think I'm sacrificing the animals for the sake of us humans, and it's true. I'm responsible for these people, Marian."

"I understand. I'm respon...I owe...in the water...that's who I'm respon...I worry..."

The situation hadn't improved when everyone settled into their bedrolls.

On the top of one of the cliffs, Marian saw two small bonfires. They...all of them, everyone...was sleeping. And some, probably for the first time in their lives, praying.

Marian had what was not much more than a flash of recognition of something called God and some process called prayer but the flash moved to a spark and then drifted off to nothing.

She went back into the dark water, to touch and glide her hands across skin and fur, to try to soothe, try to reassure. At the break of dawn, and there was more light than darkness. she came out of the water to observe the still-burning fires and to watch the great machines tearing at the walls of soil.

When breathing became too difficult, too painful, she returned to the water.

Lu, seeing progress on excavating an outlet, began to feel a little more optimistic. The plan was to start a break in the earthen wall which onrushing waters from the sea would open further, would expand into a valley of water. By nightfall, what was now a simple giant ditch should, thanks to the force of the sea, be a deep valley, a valley filled with water. And the animals now trapped in the lake could use that funnel to escape back to the sea.

In the afternoon, while everyone was fighting exhaustion, Lu walked for an hour up stony paths and trails to the top of the cliff where last night there had been the bonfires.

She introduced herself to the eight people shivering despite their heavy protective clothing. Evelyn, who introduced herself as Marian Conroy's mother, asked the first few questions, which were broken too often by sobs to be completely comprehensible. The two young men, Marian's brothers, they said, didn't ask questions, didn't even try for words; they just stood and stared down at the lake and at the figure kneeling in the water. Then a man who introduced himself as Ted thanked her for including Marian in her rescue attempt. He held his wife close against his side, and she kept shaking her head and wiping away her tears. Then Robert Conroy who, like his sons, said not a single word but was the personification of the grieving father, simply squeezed Lu's hand and turned away. A girl named Kathy, probably the same age as Marian, clung to the older of the two brothers. An older woman came forward finally, when Lu said she had to get back to the team, and said, "I'm Marian's grandmother. We've been warned that we might have to leave. It's not safe, they said. That quake last night was a warning. Tell me. Am I right in believing that Marian won't come up here as you've come up? I suspect it's a hard climb and I doubt she could make it. Does she have any messages for us?"

"I know she would want to try," Lu said. "But I also know that right now she's more worried about them than she is about you. Or us."

"About them," the old woman said. "About them. God works in wondrous ways..."

With that, the eight people huddled closer together, and Lu returned to the shore of the lake, picking her way carefully so as not to tumble over the cliff to the rocks below.

An hour later the ground shook so fiercely that the pilot of the chopper waiting up on the cliff said to his eight passengers, "Let's load up and get out of here."

Far down below the volunteers ran about in chaos for a moment until their discipline brought them, frightened but controlled, to line up at the steps leading into another chopper.

As the ground shook once more the pilot leaned out of the open door and yelled, "Let's go, let's go. Let's get out of here."

The chopper at the lake side lifted from the ground but the other chopper on the cliff waited, its blades rotating slowly.

~~~

Marian had watched the last volunteer board a chopper. She didn't know who it was. They all looked alike to her.

She kneeled in the water and held out her hand to the pup and felt her fingertips being touched by whiskers. The fingers might even have been bitten or maybe just nibbled, she couldn't be sure.

Kneeling there, Marian raised her head and saw the people...all of them...on the top of the cliff. They stood in a small group, arms around each other. She looked at each face—her mother's, her father's, Tommy's, Todd's, Kathy's, Grandma Audrey's, Ted's, Pauline's—and she struggled to find the words to complete the letter she would never send and they would never see or understand.

Words tumbled on the heels and toes of each other. She heard not word sounds but water sounds. Music sounds.

Music. Songs. Singing.

Where...ah, yes...Grandma's...Uncle Talbot's house...that CD...the whales singing, the choir...*Saint John...Divine...*

Marian saw the people on the cliff walk...*never have to walk, never again!*...walk back from the cliff, disappearing piece by piece, feet and then legs and then arms and then heads. Then Marian saw the blades of the chopper rotating faster and faster and she heard the engine roaring and she saw the chopper rise slowly into the air.

She thought at first the trembling of the earth, the trembling of the water, came from the blades and noise of the chopper but then she realized that the mounds of earth before her were shaking, were crumbling.

The sea and the earth seemed to tip and reach for each other. A rush of water swept forward and up and over her and she whose name used to be Marian knew she was being carried, along with every body in the lake, forward and down into swirling depths.

As she surfaced she saw the great walls of earth that had refused her and the others salvation in the sea settling through the dust into a flat plane. Where there were once walls and cliffs there was now only water. Only water.

water water everywhere and not...

The earth movement had thrown the lake and the sea together again, just as, days before, it had closed them off from each other.

The singing squealing trumpeting whistling huge humps were tumbled about as the seawater rushed in through the new channel. The creature who was once Marian knew, with the bit of human mind that remained, that in a moment the water would be carrying them all, every one of them, out to sea.

Swimming faster than she ever had in her eighteen years of human life, she called—to every warm body in the lake—a sound or collection of sounds that told them to follow her.

...follow me now or you will all die...follow...

They followed her.

Faster and faster they followed her through the new channel back out to the sea where they had been born and where they would live once again.

Only once did she who had once called herself...what was it she had called herself?...she had called...she looked back. As if the word might be there behind her, somewhere in the water behind her.

But she saw no words, only a metal bird in the sky.

No, not a bird...a...she could not recall the word...she saw the thing like a bird rising higher into the air and then she looked back to her family, following her.

They stirred the seawater into foam.

...good-bye ma...good-bye...good pa...pa...to...ddy...ka...gra... gra...I lov...Te...Paul...byegood...byeg...

And then, for a moment, that strange old language and those strange old faces returned and she looked into the sky and said, in words that meant nothing to the large and small ones behind her, "Grandma...God...his marvels...to per...form..."

≈

From the windows of the chopper they watched the creatures in a mighty rush pouring through the new channel. They all cheered.

They all wept.

Audrey Bishop and her daughter held hands.

Kathy, sharing a window with Todd Conroy, was crying and waving good-bye.

Tommy, sharing a window with his father, whispered, "Good-bye, Mare."

Robert Conroy, watching the long lean body leading the great flotilla of creatures out to sea, thought to himself, *we loved her and she knew that we loved her and she loved us.*

She knew that she loved us.

Didn't she know that?

Oh, please God, tell me she knew that we loved her and she knew she loved us.

Good-bye, Mare...

Good-bye, Mare...

≈

In the water, above her, a giant ray, a pair of huge white wings, glides out of the darkness. She feels the shifting layers of pressure as the great bird-like creature, all wings and luminescence, passes.

Upright columns of blood-colored beasts twist and spiral and swim with her...*serpents*...a word she knows that must mean something. Another word...*beautiful*...still has some meaning in her forever altered, still-changing mind.

Up...suddenly up...from the bottom of the sea, stirred by the great gray-black bodies moving over the seafloor, come dense clouds of...what is the *word*? The *word* that comes to mind but means nothing... *snowflakes*...Clouds of *snowflakes* that, even as they appear, are consumed by smaller and other-colored brothers and sisters.

And laughter.

Listen to the laughter in her now-world, the cold salt-sweet sea.

The word *laugh* comes to her even as the sound spills out of her. To her right and just below, a huge mother with a flip of tail, nudges her fat new baby into the sea. The baby finds long strings of—is that the word? is *kelp* the word? and what does the word *word* mean?—kelp in which to play—ah, there come the chirps and cries that together mean the word *laughter*!

Down she goes, moving through the kelp strings, over and under the baby, *laughing*...that has to be the word...with joy and pleasure.

And then she moves beneath the baby and lifts him up through the mass of water to where his giant mother receives him with milk and *kisses*...no doubt about that word, it exists in this world as it existed in the other world...with kisses on the lips of mother and son. And on the lips of this new playmate.

Leaving mother and son she swims forward through layers of water that leave in her mouth the ocean taste that is food and drink.

Now, in front of her, floating in the calm waves, is a large breathing body covered with birds plucking things...*things!*...things once called...what? ...picking things from the skin of their host.

Screaming complaints, one unwise bird stands on the twin blowholes of the huge dark gray shape and is blown skyward when sprays of steamy condensation erupt like a great fountain from those blowholes.

She floats there too in the waves and gazes up at the clouds...this is where I came from, this is where I live.

The pudgy baby whale, her playmate in the kelp moments before, glides silently beneath her and then rises to touch and lift her above the water and into the dry air and forward into the wind. As she re-enters the water, he begs her to come back and play.

When they are both exhausted, she and the baby search through the bodies crowding about them until, finding the patient mother, they settle beside her, one on either side of her, their bodies touching hers.

They move through the sea as one body, singing to the sea, the sky, and the stars.

The End

About Mermaids

"David Thompson, to whom an Orkney islander related a colorful version of the story, quotes his informants as saying that when Brita bore her children, their fingers and toes were *'webbed like the paws o' a selchie.'* The midwife clipped the membrane between each finger and toe, a task which their mother had to perform many times as the children grew up, otherwise the fins would have grown together again. After many generations the webbed fingers and toes resolved themselves into the horny excrescence by which the *'men wi' the horns on their hands and feet'* may be recognized as the descendants of Brita."

"THE PEOPLE OF THE SEA" FROM *SEA ENCHANTRESS*
BENWELL, GWEN AND ARTHUR WAUGH, LONDON, 1961

～

"...They were forever seeing a woman on the point, and they knew it was the mermaid that was ever living in the river, and one day the man saw her sitting on a big stone on the point and she a-combing her fine golden hair back from the forehead of her, and combing it from the rack. And he faced round and crept up behind her when she was not knowing it, and caught her by the two shoulders of her, and brought her to his house, where his mother lived."

"THE SHANNON MERMAID" FROM *THE GAEL*,
NOVEMBER, 1899, P.238 NEW YORK,

DETAILED IN *A TREASURE OF IRISH FOLKLORE*,
ED. BY PADRAIC COLUM, BONANZA, 1983

～

"The Mermaid Seen on the Coast of Caithness.

Dear Sir, About twelve years ago, when I was a Parochial Schoolmaster at Reay, in the course of my walking on the shore of Sandside Bay, being a warm fine day in summer, I was induced to extend my walk towards Sandside Head, when my attention was arrested by the appearance of a figure resembling an unclothed human female, sitting upon a rock....The forehead was round, the face plump, the cheeks ruddy, the eyes blue, the mouth and lips of a natural form....the breasts and abdomen, the arms and fingers of the size of a full grown body of the human species. It remained on the rock three or four minutes after I observed it, and was exercised during that period in combing its hair, which was long and thick, and of which it appeared proud, and then dropped into the sea, from which it did not reappear to me.

(Signed) Wm. Munro"

LETTER WRITTEN TO *THE TIMES* OF LONDON
BY WILLIAM MUNRO, A SCHOOLMASTER, IN 1809

〜

An English law, still on the books in the 19th century, officially claimed for the Crown "all mermaids found in British waters."

〜

"Just as animals can hear notes in the musical register which the human ear cannot comprehend, so man is dimly aware of meaningful music which transcends his experience and which yet—irritating thought—may have held more meaning to his less traffic-drowned civilized ancestors of, say, 800 B.C. So, siren music may mean death; but it may also be a window opening on the eternal and the unknown."

"THE PEOPLE OF THE SEA" FROM *SEA ENCHANTRESS*
BENWELL, GWEN AND ARTHUR WAUGH, LONDON, 1961

〰

"…'The 18th of November 1565 we came to Thora, which Citie is on the shoare of the sea of the Red Sea of no lustrue; the Haven small, in which ships laden with Spices out of Arabia, Abassia, and India resort. In this Citie wee saw a mermaids skinne taken there many years before, which in the lower part ends Fish-fashion: of the upper part, onely the Navill and Breasts remaine; the arms and head being lost…"

*PURCHAS, HIS PILGRIMAGE OR RELATIONS OF THE WORLD
AND THE RELIGIONS OBSERVED IN ALL AGES AND PLACES
DISCOVERED FROM THE CREATION UNTO THIS PRESENT
VOL. 2 BY SAMUEL PURCHAS, 1617*

*QUOTED FROM THE FOURE JOURNALS OF BREIDENBACH,
BELLONIUS AND CHRISTOPHER FURER OF HAIMENDORS*

〰

"We have never seen a porpoise 'go berserk' and attack a human with persistence as a dog or a horse may do. One gains the subjective impression that the porpoise is a firm, fair disciplinarian, exhibiting just as much aggression as will serve its purpose and no more. A female rough-toothed porpoise, mother of a hybrid calf, was kept alone in a tank with her calf and frequently solicited stroking from her trainer. The calf occasionally situated itself between mother and trainer while the mother was being stroked. When the calf was approximately a month old, the trainer in this situation one day stroked the calf. The mother swung her tail from the water, reached up and out, and struck the trainer a sharp, but not damaging, blow across the shoulders, and then with no further apparent anger continued to solicit stroking for herself."

Pryor, Karen W.
"Behavior and Learning in Porpoises and Whales,"
Naturwissenschaften 1973

"When I was a boy living in a village two days journey from Ayacucho my uncle saw a mermaid by the waterfall. The whole family went immediately to make offerings to her so that trouble would not fall on my uncle. We left her food, always pair—male and female—and other presents. Whoever sees a mermaid is afraid because she foretells of misfortune. Sometimes the bad luck can be stopped if the offerings are made soon enough."

REPORTED CONVERSATION WITH NICARIO JIMENEZ
AYACUCHO, PERU

≈

"This morning one of our companie looking over boord saw a Mermaid...from Navill upward, her back and breasts were like a woman's (as they say who saw her) her body as big as one of us; her skin very white; and long haire hanging down behinde, of color blacke; in her going downe they saw her tayle, which was like the tayle of a porposse and speckled like a Macrell."

FROM HENRY HUDSON'S LOGBOOK, JUNE 15, 1608
"MYTHS AND MERMAIDS"
WOMEN AND THE SEA
THE MARINERS' MUSEUM, NEWPORT NEWS, VIRGINIA

≈

In Hans Christian Andersen's fairy tale, "The Little Mermaid," every young mermaid was permitted, on her fifteenth birthday, to rise from her palace under the sea to the surface...

This is the story of a special mermaid.

"When her turn came, she saw what the others had not seen the first time they went up. The sea looked quite green, and large icebergs were floating about, each of the most singular shape that glittered like diamonds. She had seated herself upon one of the largest and let the wind played with her long hair, and she remarked that all the ships...steered as far away as they could from the iceberg, as if they were afraid of it. Towards evening, as the sun went down, dark clouds covered the sky, the thunder rolled and the lightning flashed, and the red light glowed on the icebergs as they rocked and tossed on the heaving sea. On all the ships the sails were reefed with fear and trembling, while she sat calmly on the floating iceberg, watching the blue lightning as it darted its forked flashes into the sea."

In 1909, entranced by a ballet based on the 1837 Andersen story, Carl Jacobsen, a Danish brewer, commissioned the sculptor Edvard Erikson to create a bronze statue of the mermaid. In 1913, the mermaid, "Den Lille Havfrue" was installed on a rock in the water at Langelinie quay in Copenhagen.

And she sits there on her rock to this day, calmly facing the sea, a beloved symbol of Denmark.

♒

Afterword

Several years ago, when I was chief x-ray technician at Alta Bates Hospital in Berkeley, I was called by a nurse in the delivery room and informed that a stillborn infant was being brought to the department for x-ray examination.

The nurse arrived, carrying the blanket-wrapped bundle in her arms. She placed it on the table and unwrapped the blanket. The baby, a female, had a normal upper torso, but her lower torso consisted of one long tapering set of legs joined together at the ankles. The feet were divided at the ankle and splayed out. The toes, like the fingers, were joined by thick webbing. This phenomenon is known as syndactyly.

The skin of the upper torso was smooth, the skin of the lower torso was very coarse. The radiologist, Dr. William Picard, examined the x-rays, returned them to their envelope and on the front of the envelope he wrote the word mermaid .

Three weeks later the same nurse brought another stillborn infant for x-rays. This time the baby, a male, was a perfect Cyclops. He had a single eye in the center of his forehead. The radiologist examined the films and wrote on the envelope the single word Cyclops.

Some years later, as a professor at Saint Mary's College of California, my students and I read and discussed Homer's *Odyssey*, recited and written thousands of years ago. The Odyssey contained a chapter titled "Island of the Cyclopes." In another chapter the hero Odysseus orders himself lashed to the mast of his ship so he might resist the beautiful sirens calling from the waves. Illustrations, ancient and contemporary, show sirens to be mermaids.

To provoke such images some women must have given birth to a baby mermaid and a baby cyclops. Could one or more of either have survived? Given the advances in medical research, the mermaid and the cyclops I x-rayed might have survived were they born today.

As Marian survived.

Chester Aaron

Author Biography

Chester Aaron has been an x-ray technician and an English professor, and is a well know grower of gourmet garlic in California. But most of all, he is a writer. Several of his young-adult and adult novels will soon be available as audio-books. Several of his prize-winning books for young adults have been honored by the New York Public Library and the National Society of Social Workers, one was a selection of the Junior Literary Guild, and one became a 90-minute ABC-TV weekend special.

For many years Aaron has been a supporter of the environment and a volunteer in marine mammal rescue efforts. His volunteer work in one rescue, of a Humpback whale trapped in the Sacramento River, brings authenticity to the sea mammal rescues in HOME TO THE SEA.

If you'd like to write to him, his e-mail address is: cgar@sonic.net.